MERRY TRAPMAS

ICE & FROST

MIA SKY

URBAN AINT DEAD

URBAN AINT DEAD
P.O Box 448
Maybrook, NY 12543

All rights reserved. Published by URBAN AINT DEAD Publications.

Cover Design: P. Wise / The Wise Services

Edited By: Artessa Michele-Thomas / Editing 01

Contact Author on FB: Tha PenGoddess / IG: @thepengoddess

Contact Publisher at www.urbanaintdead.com

Email: urbanaintdead@gmail.com

Print ISBN: 979-8-9888415-5-5

CONTENTS

SOUNDTRACKS

Scan the QR Code below to listen to the Soundtracks/Singles of some of your favorite U.A.D titles:

Don't have Spotify or Apple Music?
No Sweat!
Visit your choice streaming platform and search URBAN AINT DEAD.

Currently on lock serving a bid?
JPay, iHeartRadio, WHATEVER!
We got you covered.

Simply log into your facility's kiosk or tablet, go to music and
search URBAN AINT DEAD.

URBAN AINT DEAD

Like & Follow us on social media:
FB - URBAN AINT DEAD
IG: @urbanaintdead
Tik Tok - @urbanaintdead

SUBMISSIONS

Submit the first three chapters of your completed manuscript to urbanaintdead@gmail.com, subject line: Your book's title. The manuscript must be in a .doc file and sent as an attachment. The document should be in Times New Roman, double-spaced, and in size 12 font. Also, provide your synopsis and full contact information. If sending multiple submissions, they must each be in a separate email. Have a story but no way to submit it electronically? You can still submit to URBAN AINT DEAD. Send in the first three chapters, written or typed, of your completed manuscript to:

URBAN AINT DEAD
P.O Box 448
Maybrook, NY 12543

DO NOT send original manuscript. Must be a duplicate.
Provide your synopsis and a cover letter containing your full contact information.
Thanks for considering URBAN AINT DEAD.

~ *DEDICATION*~

I dedicate this book to my brother, Arnold. May you rest in peace and continue shining down on me.

ICE CITY, CALIFORNIA

It was my first night dancing at this local after-hours event. It was held at a secret location and you had to know somebody that knew somebody just to get the location. When scamming became a slow hustle for me, I had to figure something else out and it was either selling pussy or shaking ass. Shaking ass was the choice for me. With my record, there was no way a nine to five would hire my ass. Besides, I had no choice but shake this mothafucka. There was no way I'd choose prostitution. Being a single mother of a little girl, I had to do what I needed to do. Christmas was approaching, and I was very much behind on my mortgage and car notes. I lived a very lavish lifestyle and required a certain type of income to maintain it. Struggling with my four-year-old wasn't an option and holding my hand out wasn't either.

I tossed back the shot of Tequila, allowing it to relax me. This was my very first stage set, and the encouragement of my best friend, Cristal, led me here. She'd danced at the events prior to her pregnancy and always told me how good the money was. As long as it came quickly, nothing else really mattered to me. I sprayed the glitter on my honey golden skin and rubbed it in. After coating my lips with my NYX butter gloss and brushing the forty-inch bundles straight, I looked in the mirror and made sure my look was giving.

Being the baddest bitch in the room was intimidating to some; I didn't too much give a fuck though. These bitches and their botched BBL bodies weren't fucking with me. I had the deepest dimples and an enticing smile. My body was completely natural, thanks to my firstborn child for keeping me thick. Waist was slim as hell, tits were perky, and this ass moved like water. When your confidence was through the roof like mine, mothafuckas felt that shit. In an environment like this, you had no friends; everybody was a opp.

"Ice, you're up in two minutes!" Debbie shouted into the dressing room. Debbie was the house mom. She was responsible for making sure all of the girls stayed in line and was on time to their stage sets.

"Thanks Debbie," I responded before walking out of the dressing room. After making my way out of the dressing room, I stepped onto the main stage as the DJ introduced me by my stage name, which was Ice. The men in the crowd hollered and cheered for me to come do my thing. Saying I wasn't nervous would be a lie; I wasn't anywhere near ready for this lifestyle, but it wasn't any turning back now. It was too late.

The sounds of music blared through the speakers. I began to tune out everything around me, feeling nothing but the beat. For the next three minutes, I owned the building, selling the fantasy to all these niggas. By the time the music ended, the stage was covered in ones. There was three rules to this game: when the money stop, you stop dancing, never trust a bitch and, lastly, no fucking customers. Those were rules I didn't mind abiding by. The sweeper came out and bagged my money; I didn't have to work the floor at all the way I was racked up.

"Good job new booty," Debbie complimented, passing me the bag of money.

"Thanks Deb," I replied, taking the bag from her hands. After doing my count, I tipped the sweeper and paid the owner my house fee for the night. I walked out of there with three-thousand dollars; I couldn't be mad at that. Three thousand was a lot of money for my first night. My daughter was going to have a great Christmas and I was going to make sure of it.

THE NEXT DAY...

"Mommy wakey!" Kiara hollered, jumping on my bed. It

had to be every bit of seven in the morning, and this little girl had nothing but energy. Meanwhile, I was tired as shit.

"Good morning baby." I yawned.

"Mommy, I want pancakes." Kiara smiled.

I smothered her in kisses. My daughter would never know the word 'No'; it wasn't in my vocabulary when it came to her. My daughter had everything I didn't have and, by all means, I'd make sure it remained that way.

"Alright, baby, pancakes it is," I responded while getting out of bed. Sliding on my slippers and robe, I picked Kiara up and we headed straight to the kitchen. Sitting her down at the kiddie table, I placed her iPad in front of her. She loved watching little cartoons while I cooked.

Skimming the refrigerator, I made a mental note to go out and grocery shop. We had little to no food but, as a mother, we turned nothing into something. Eggs, sausage, and pancakes as requested for my princess. I sat her plate in front of her, and she smiled from ear to ear.

"Thank you, mommy." Kiara smiled, stuffing her face with food.

"You welcome baby," I responded.

I made enough money to pay my rent, but I still had other expenses to cover. The roof over me and my daughter's head was more important than anything else. I was on a money mission for the next two weeks. As long as we were good, life was good. Once Kiara finished her meal, I got her dressed and myself.

We had mountains of errands to run, and I had to find her a daycare. My mama was awol; she barely was around for me growing up, so my expectations of her being present in my daughter's life was slim to none. My baby's father died shortly after my daughter was born. When I lost him, my whole world sunk. Depression took me over, and his mother stepped in and became my support system. She was the mother I never had and the grandmother Kiara needed. That was a full blessing. She was open to watching Kiara during the night, and I used daycare for mornings mostly when I needed to get something done or needed a mommy break. Kiara was in good hands no matter which route I took; she was a very good child and hardly ever got into trouble. To be fair, she was four years old and still learning right from wrong. My daughter was very smart and advanced though; she had the mouth of a forty-year-old. Most times I'd ask her if she was four, fourteen, or forty. Kiara was my mini me for sure, with an attitude and sass like her mother.

"Are you ready to go?" I questioned.

"Yeah mama! Can we go get Starbucks?" Kiara asked with a smile planted across her cute face.

"Of course we can, baby," I answered. Locking up the house, I put my baby in her car seat and pushed start my 2022 Mercedes Benz C300.

"Can you play my song mama? You know that song that you are playing," Kiara's little voice was questioned.

I chuckled and turned on the radio, blasting *Favorite Song* by Toosii. She loved that song and made me play it every chance she got. One thing about my little baby was that she loved music and she loved to sing and dance. I wanted my girl to go to ballet classes, that would be the next thing on the to-do list. She'd jump around the house and do twirls and spins all day. Once the bag was right, she would definitely be doing every activity she pleased.

The drive to the bank was short. We made it within twelve minutes. I grabbed Kiara and my purse before entering. I needed to make a cash deposit into my account and a money order to pay the rent. I didn't have every dime that I needed to get my rent caught up but I had enough to keep my landlord quiet for another week. If I stuck to my plan for the next couple of weeks, things would fall alright. The line in the bank was long as hell; it seemed like everybody and their mama was in here today. The lady in front of me reeked horribly. Her body smelled of onions and must. I didn't understand how people were hella musty during the winter. There wasn't any heat out, like what was your excuse? Wear deodorant and wash your ass, simple.

"Next in line!" a teller called out.

The funky woman moved up, causing the line to move faster. Kiara had a funny look on her face as though she smelled the exact same thing that I did.

Silently, I chuckled at her scrunched up face. "Fix your face Kiara," I demanded.

"It stank mama," she whined.

"I know baby, some people just don't practice good hygiene," I replied.

"But why mama? We take baths every day," she responded.

"There's some people in this world like us and some that aren't. You have met a lot of people in this world that are nothing like you and I babygirl...we all ain't cut from the same cloth," I explained.

"Okay mama," she responded.

"Next in line!" a different teller called out.

We moved up and, the moment we made it to the teller's booth, the lady smiled at Kiara. "She is too adorable," she complimented.

"Kiara, what do you say?" I smiled, questioning Kiara. One thing I didn't play about was respect and manners. My daughter had to learn early what it meant to be respectful to adults and people in general. I wasn't raising any mean girls.

"Thank you!" she replied excitedly.

"You're welcome beautiful… I'm Jenny, I'll be your teller today. How may I assist you?" she questioned, turning her attention back towards me.

"Hi Jenny, I'm here to make a deposit today.," I answered while passing my I.D. and debit card.

"No problem, how much will you be depositing today ma'am?" she questioned, punching my information into the computer system.

"I'll be depositing two thousand in my account and I'd like to get a seventeen-hundred-dollar money order as well," I replied.

"Okay, will that be a cash or check deposit?" she questioned.

"This will be a cash deposit," I replied, taking the stacks of one-hundred-dollar bills and placing them in front of her. As she began counting it out, I caught a bitch staring at me. I noticed her from the club last night. I ain't giving that bitch not one smirk or smile. She mugged the shit out of me, and I knew exactly why. I made the biggest bag on a stage set and the envy was there. Shit was regular for me; I wasn't stunting no bitch. The teller printed the money order out and gave me my deposit receipt. I felt good inside knowing that I accomplished something today. I had my rent paid down; it wasn't the full amount but it was something. I kept my word to my landlord and that bought me enough time to get another bag to pay off some more.

FROSTY

RICH CITY, CALIFORNIA

Mocha bobbed her head up and down for about twenty minutes straight and still didn't get me off. A nigga was going limp in her jaws, and I was over it. The head was just as wack as her pussy and, honestly, I didn't want it. Grabbing her hair and pulling her off me, I motioned for her to stop.

"Why do I gotta stop bae?" she questioned, raising her eyebrows.

"Man, what did I tell you about that bae shit? You gotta stop cus that head boring mama," I answered. It was no point of lying; she should've been able to tell by the way my shit went limp.

"Well, can I at least give you some pussy?" she whispered.

"Nah, pack it up and dip," I replied, buckling my pants. This bop was useless; she ain't have shit to offer me besides coochie and bad vibes.

"Fuck you, nigga," she spat.

A response was something she wasn't going to receive from me. I ain't give a flying fuck about how she felt; she wasn't my girl. I met Mocha two years ago at an after-hours event. She was the baddest in there at the time. She had a banging ass body and the nicest pair of lips my dick had ever met. We would do whatever we wanted together and have life our way. She stuck around and held be down when I needed her to, and her loyalty wasn't something I had to question. Mocha was an down ass bitch, ready for whatever.

Our relationship shifted drastically when she started doing coke. That was some shit that didn't seem attractive to me. I ain't want no woman powdering her nose in front of me or even stealing it from me. The rule of this game was never get high off your own supply, and trusting a coke head wasn't in my deck of cards. Everything about her changed; she depended on the snow. She needed the shit to function. Her body was changing and so was her attitude.

Mocha wasn't my lil' boo anymore; she was now just a bitch that I fucked from time to time. Even then, the fucking was getting tiring. I didn't even want the bitch near me.

"Why you still here?" I asked, staring her from head to toe.

"So, you really gonna put me out?" she questioned. I didn't bother answering because I said all that was needed. She needed to get the point and go before I became a bigger asshole towards her silly ass.

"Whatever, can I get a bump then?" she questioned.

It was a question floating in my head if this bitch was really bold enough to ask me for some snow. She knew I would never sell that shit to her or allow her to even partake in some shit like this in front of me. I was really done with Mocha's smoked-out ass.

"Don't ask me no weird ass shit like that; you'll never in your life get no form of drugs from me. Take yo ass on before I fire off on yo ass," I responded. She knew I meant business, and that was something to stand on.

Quickly, she put on her clothing and slid out the door. That bitch moved so quickly up out of my house; she must've felt my energy shift. I scrolled through my phone and clicked on the Instagram app. It was a ton of videos being reposted of a dancer working the pole. She was raw as hell, beautiful, and mesmerizing. I'd never seen her before, so I knew she had to be new or from out the way.

The caption on the page read "Ice the coldest". In fact, she was the coldest pole worker I'd seen in a while. I clicked on the tagged page and it took me straight to her page.

Baby was a dime piece, slim waist, and a fat ass. By the looks of the tiger stripes on her booty, I could tell that she was all natural. It had been a while since I saw a natural woman. It seemed as though everybody and their mom had a BBL.

After lurking her page, I made a mental note to see her in person.

My burner phone began going off, indicating that there was a drop ready to be picked up. I texted my right-hand man, letting him know I was on my way to the trap. I grabbed the keys to my all-black G-Wagon and my Glock Forty. It was necessary to stay strapped. I was a Southside nigga and we were the most hated in this city, yet so respected.

Hopping into my car, I turned on the radio, blasting my old school playlist. Mac Dre slapped through the speakers, as I cruised slow through the cold streets. I loved my city, but it was dangerous. I stayed out here only twice a week to ensure business continued running smoothly. I resided in Oakland Hills. It was more upscale and suburban than the hood neighborhoods. I lived in a nice four-bedroom home; I had no kids and no desire to have any.

At the age of twenty-nine, I was having life my way. I enjoyed getting money and blowing it on myself or ducking off. Sometimes, I did get lonely but, for the most part, taking trips and fucking bitches got rid of that void. I know it suppressed temporary time, but it was something I did from time. Don't get me wrong, being in a relationship and growing with someone was something that crossed my mind periodically. For this moment, it was whatever it's going to be. When the Most High wanted to bless me with love, he would. As for now, I was chilling and catching plays.

Pulling up to the trap spot, I parked my car and locked the doors. Everybody around the Crest knew who I was;

these apartments were where I came up. My mom moved to Crescent Park before I was born, and we lived here until I was eighteen. This neighborhood watched me grow from a corner boy to the head honcho. They labeled me as a hood hero, not because of me selling drugs. I gave back to this community the moment that I was able to. I fed the homeless folks on this block and gave back to single mothers. Whenever anybody needed protection or something for their babies, they came to me. It wasn't anything I minded either.

My mom was a single mother, and I witnessed her struggling to take care of me. So, as long as I was able, it would be all good for the neighborhood moms. A lot of people judged me and held me accountable for the drugs that were on the streets. To be truthful, that shit been out here since before I was born. Why judge me? I was just a young nigga with a family to feed.

"Wassup Young?" I greeted, walking through the apartment door. It was four niggas inside and two bitches. One nigga cooked up while the females bagged up. I had a nigga on security and another one counting money.

"What's good Frost? We almost done counting up," Rali spoke as he whipped up on the stove.

"On a serious tip, any of them young niggas had a problem paying up this week?" I questioned. There were a few young dudes I had selling for me. They were still in high school and, when payday came around, it was always an excuse.

This game was a grown man's game; I didn't need no child play. I gave them a chance because I knew how it was being you with no shine. Growing up in a single-parent household and watching your mother struggle was tough. Growing up in the hood was basically survival. Most dudes from the Bay Area didn't make it to see eighteen, twenty-one, or even twenty-five. If you did, you were considered an OG, and that's sad. My cousin, Toonkie, died when we were fifteen years old. He was shot while riding his bike. He wasn't even in the streets; I was though, and he rolled with me, so I always felt guilty for his death. That shit was on me.

"Nah, they dropped early Frosty. I was surprised," G-Man chuckled.

"Niggas ain't got a choice; it's the holiday season. Motherfuckers have to fall in line," Rali responded.

He ain't lying; they didn't have a choice. Taking away from me was taking away from the next man. Everybody got a purpose in this game and that was to get money and provide. People had families and bills; this dirty money did a lot good and a lot bad.

"If you have any problems, let me know." I grinned, grabbing the duffel bag from the table. It was heavy just the way I liked it to be.

I SPRAYED ON MY ARMANI COLOGNE AND PUT ON MY CARTIER glasses along with two gold chains. The bust down was to a minimum tonight. A flashy nigga was something that I wasn't but, on occasion, it was a slight possibly I'd show off. It was a chill night for me though.

I grabbed the keys to my chrome Audi RS6 before heading out. It was one of my favorite cars; the G-Wagon was my first baby. I smelled like money and looked like it too. It was a celebration night for me and my niggas, so we had to blow a bag. Of course, we were hitting the after-hours. Seeing this new girl Ice and her talent was a part of my to-do list. I wanted to see what the hype was about.

Before I pushed the start button on my ignition, my phone began ringing; it was Mocha's ass, of course. Her washed up ass been calling me since I made her leave my crib. She had nothing that I'd want and me wanting her to understand that shit was basically a dream. Fucking with Mocha was becoming a nightmare. I was overly tired of her harassing me. I knew the bitch was hardheaded but I didn't think she was that stubborn. She didn't give up no matter how bad I talked to her. It was weird as hell to me.

I cruised down the streets of Oakland making each turn until I made it to the after-hours spot. After parking my car, I headed straight to the entrance. Standing in line wasn't something I did, ever. Niggas knew me and respected me; I was presidential around here. "What's goodie?" I greeted SB, one of the bouncers.

"What's good Brodie? Yo V.I.P. section is ready," he replied.

"Fasho," I said before stepping in the club. I saw a few of my niggas were already comfortable, popping bottles and vibing to the music. It was lit as fuck and the women were bad as hell. I looked around and noticed the baddie from Instagram walking towards the back in a sweatsuit.

Approaching my booth, I greeted my niggas and sat my duffel full of ones on the table. Before I knew it, bottle girls were entering with Ace of Spade. It was boss shit only, every time. We were taking shots of different alcohol and smoking fat blunts. Two bitches came to the section, I knew one of them.

Cream used to roll with Mocha back in the day. She was a boujee ass white bitch from Riverbank. She and Mocha were two peas in a pod at one point. They were an dynamic duo but, of course, females in the game never remained solid to one another. Never knowing the details of what happened between them, fingers were pointed at Mocha.

"Wassup Frosty? You want a dance papi?" Cream questioned with eyes full of lust. This girl been wanting to fuck me. When she and Mocha were close, she would give me the same look.

"I'm good love." I smiled, still tipping her. She wasn't ugly and her body was banging; however, I didn't want no dance from any of Mocha's little minions. That shit was messy considering how close they once were.

"Damn alright," Cream scoffed.

As she began to walk away, I grabbed her by her arm. "Tell that new chick I want a private dance," I requested, pulling a stack out the duffel and placing it in her hand.

"Say less," she responded with her eyes big as day. With no hesitation, she walked straight to the back of the club.

ICELYNN

Slowly, I brushed my hair, making sure each strand laid perfectly. The look had to be on point. It was packed and, after the stage set on my first night, I just knew it was moncy was on the floor tonight. I wore a pink, rhinestone fishnet lingerie set along with my peep-toe platform heels and my hair in a high ponytail with some down in the back.

"Aye, new booty… you're wanted in the V.I.P. section. It's some money out there girl," one of the dancers said.

"Who me?" I questioned; it was other new dancers besides me.

"Girl yes! Your name is Ice, right?" she questioned.

"Yes, what's your name?" I questioned.

"Cream, nice to meet you, girly! Now, go get your money before the next bitch get it for ya," she answered.

I nodded my head before tossing back another shot of Hennessy VSOP. Taking a deep breath, I walked onto the dance floor. The club smelled like nothing but weed, dollar bills, and a combination of cheap fragrances. The song *Thick Bitch* by Bandgang was playing and all the big booty girls were acting up on stage, and I loved that for them.

As I made my way to the V.I.P. section, an older guy stopped me for a dance. He held up four crisp hundred dollar bills. Before I could accept or deny his request, security called my name and motioned for me walk over to the section.

"I'm sorry love, next time," I ensured the guy while strutting my way to the V.I.P. booth.

"Frosty requested you," Chuck, the security guard, notified me as he stepped to the side, giving me access to walk through.

Strutting my way to the section, my eyes met the finest piece of chocolate life had to offer. His eyes were fixated onto me as mine was on him. His mouth was full of gold, his locs hung past his shoulders, and he had the deepest pair of dimples I'd ever seen. If handsome was a person, it was him. The aura screamed alpha, boss, and finer than a mothafucka. I just knew that God took his time on this man.

"Wassup lil mama?" he questioned.

"You must be Frosty," I answered seductively.

"I am. Ice, right?" He questioned. He was acting like he knew me. All these men knew my name in this club. I was the coldest new girl on the line up.

I could tell that he was curious. As a lot of niggas were, I was exclusive. "Yup," I said, popping the 'P'.

"Can I get a private dance?" He questioned.

"Sure, one hundred dollars entry and a two-song minimum," I answered. He pulled out two stacks.

"Money good mamas," he chuckled.

As long as the money was flowing, I was dancing. I motioned for him to follow me and as expected, he did. The scent of his cologne enticed me. The shoes on his feet said a lot too, but the watch on his wrist let me know he was paid. We entered the blue room; it had mirrors covering every wall. The room was lit in blue lights with a nice sectional sofa which was white and plush. The pole stood in the center of the lavender scented room. It was a whole vibe in there.

Before entering, he was to pay an entry fee. Instead of giving me a single one-hundred-dollar bill, he gave me four. The song *Put It Down* by T-Pain blasted, and I began to start working the pole. I climbed to the very top and did a few spins before coming down into a split. I felt his eyes glued to me, but I never looked into them.

Something about his presence gave me a sense of security. I felt safe in his presence and that was an odd feeling to have. I continued dancing and, before I knew it, the song changed to *Freakin You* by Jodeci. I made my way to his lap and began grinding on him. My hips whined and rotated, as he smacked and grabbed my ass cheeks.

"You too beautiful to be fucking around in this club." He sighed, pulling out another stack of money to throw at me.

"Who are you to tell me where I belong?" I questioned.

"Frosty, I'm that nigga, baby," he answered in confidence.

"Well, I'm Ice baby, and I don't like when a nigga think he can reroute and redirect my decisions," I responded. I didn't care how fine he was; ain't no nigga telling me where, what, how, and when, especially one that didn't belong to me.

"Independent, I like that," he chuckled.

"Very, times up baby love. Thanks for having me." I smiled, strutting out the room as Lazlo entered to sweep my money. Lazlo was a tall, skinny, and cockeyed dude from around the way. He was also one of the security guards here at the club.

I made my way to the locker room; it was time to change and freshen up before my stage set. Security handed me my money bag from the private dance, and I shoved it into my locker before locking it up. Trusting a bunch of females that had given me nothing but ugly stares since I'd stepped foot in this club wasn't a part of my to-do list. Trust was to be earned, not given.

I looked in the mirror, infatuated with myself. The beauty I held was rare. A lot of bitches in this club would just stare, some with eyes full of lust and some of envy. I didn't come here for friends though; the money was my reason.

If it wasn't for the way life had been beating my ass, I honestly wouldn't even be here. Drinking was a must every time I stepped foot into this club. I couldn't be sober dealing with the stares and the energies that came with it. This was a job. I sold a fantasy and, by the end of the day, I was back home with my child living my regular life. She was my purpose and reason, and I'd never allow her to go without.

"Ice, you ready?" Debbie questioned.

"I am," I replied, standing from my seat. As always, smelling like Prada and looking like the bag I wanted to make, I walked my ass straight to the stage ready to perform.

Tossing back a shot of Casamigo, I took a deep ass breath while the DJ introduced me to the stage. *Milk Marie* by Young Thug blasted through the speakers. I had a thing for slow dancing and tonight that was the vibe. I had a two-song set tonight. It was another lit ass night in the club; it was so many familiar and unfamiliar faces in the building. I was finally feeling those shots and began dancing and moving my body. I was full of tricks tonight and the trick of the night was fire. Grabbing the candle, I slid it into my pussy and grabbed a can of hair spray. I lit the candle and sprayed the hair spray towards the flames.

The crowd began going wild. Money was covering the stage, and I continued dancing and teasing the crowd. It was nothing but energy coming from them; they cheered and turned me up. I climbed to the top of the pole and spun all the way down clacking my heels. Just like that, I made some money; I was ending my night on a good note. When the money was made, the bills were paid.

THE NEXT DAY...

The alarm was blaring, waking me right out of the little cat nap I took. It felt like my eyes were closed for five minutes and then, I was abruptly interrupted. There was a lot to do on my agenda today, starting off with getting the rest of these bills out the way and getting my daughter enrolled in an extracurricular activity. I needed her to be in whatever form of activities she wanted to be in. Once I was fully woken up, I checked on my daughter. She was still asleep in her room, which gave me enough time to take a hot shower and prepare for the day.

Hopping in the shower, I lathered my body with my favorite body wash and cleaned it from head to toe. After twenty minutes of handling my hygiene, I laid out an all-black bodycon dress and an acid wash jean jacket, along with an pair of sandals to match. I was going for a cute comfy look for the day. Parting my hair down the middle, I decided on doing two simple French braids on each side of my head. It was a no makeup type of day, just lashes and lip gloss.

"Kiara, baby, wake up! Today is out day sunshine." I smiled while kissing Kiara all over her face, trying to wake her up.

She laid there smiling with her eyes close, pretending to be asleep. "Mommy's favorite girl gets pancakes from IHOP!" I added, tickling her.

She began to laugh. "Cake cakes with strawberries mama?" Kiara asked.

"Yup, and whipped cream! That's how you like it princess," I answered.

"Yay mommy, can I pick my clothes today? I'm a big girl," Kiara questioned.

"Sure, but go brush your teeth first," I answered, scrunching up my face and holding my nose.

"My breath not stinky mommy," Kiara pouted.

"It is so gone and brush that dragon breath," I chuckled, as she stood up and went straight into the restroom. I followed behind her to ensure that she got herself together properly.

One thing about me was I made sure that I taught my daughter how to properly take care of herself. As a mother, it was my duty to make sure she grew into the respectable young woman that I knew she could be. The one that I wanted her to be was fearless, confident, independent, and strong. I made sure she saw me at my best so that she always had an example of what a strong black woman looked like.

Kiara picked out a pair of jean overalls and a white tank top with her all-white Converse to match. My little baby had some flavor already, and I loved that for her. When she was all dressed and ready to go, we headed out the door. Before we did anything, I made sure that my daughter ate first. Breakfast was the most important meal of the day and nourishing our bodies was a healthy habit.

It took us literally fifteen minutes to make it where we needed to go. My daughter loved her a fresh stack of pancakes and scrambled eggs. She didn't care for anything else when it came to IHOP. The waiter seated us at our booth and gave us both a menu. Kiara had a few colored crayons and began doodling on the color in child's menu. I already knew what we both wanted.

"Can I start you two off with some drinks?" the waiter questioned.

"Yes, can we start with orange juice and a glass of apple

juice? Also, I'd like to proceed with my food order," I answered.

"Sure thing, what would you like?" he questioned.

"I'd like the steak omelet and a side order of hash browns and, for my princess, can we have a small stack of pancakes and scrambled eggs with cheese?" I requested.

"No problem," he replied, writing down my order. After reading it back to me to make sure the order was right, he walked away.

Kiara sat there drawing and singing songs from the Frozen movie while I scrolled through my Instagram feed. My notifications were lit the hell up. Another video of me going viral and, this time, I was going to use that shit to my advantage. The thought of me taking bookings and becoming a model and dancing at parties traveled through my mind. Dancing was only temporary until a bigger blessing came.

"Short stack for the little misses and omelet for the mama," the server announced, placing our plates in front of us.

"Thank you." I smiled.

"Yummy, thank you!" Kiara said excitedly.

Kiara and I ate our food and enjoyed every bite of it. The best bonding moments in the world was priceless. Kiara lit my whole world up no matter how dark the days got. Her little smile gave me hope for better days.

FROSTY

My encounter with Ice was interesting. She had a boss ass attitude and an energy that showed she didn't play that shit. Her independence was everything, and I could tell that her head was strong. Icelynn was a talented woman, but I wanted to know who she was outside of the strip club. I wanted to get to know her as a person and see her being herself, not the persona she put up at work.

She seemed to have a decent head on her shoulders and, hopefully, she didn't allow the fast life to pollute her mind. Once the liquor and drugs started coming into play, didn't shit else matter. Your whole life was going downhill and, once every bitch had access to you, the value you once had was taken away. However, I got a whole different vibe from Ice. Her aura was giving off something I somewhat craved.

Most women would easily fall to my feet, yet she didn't. The whole Bay Area knew who I was, and she wasn't even fazed by my status. Those were the type of things I looked at. I didn't want no female that any nigga had easy access to base on his social status or net worth. That wasn't the energy I needed around me; I had enough of that fucking with Mocha's ass. A woman with some class and a good head on her shoulders was a woman for me. All my life, it was women wanting me because I had the income and ran shit in the city. Bitches wanted to fuck and get tricked on. It wasn't Halloween; I ain't had no tricks for nobody's treat. When a female never asked for shit, it made me want to give her nothing but the world and some.

I needed a woman who was willing to be my peace and nothing more. I dealt with the streets and risked my life every day. Shit, being the type of nigga who could lose his life at any given moment, I was determined to feel constant love and love endlessly. Growing up in environments full of broken love, you never get to see the healthy example of the genuine pain free safe love. That was something that I wanted to build within the right partner. Fast life was cool but, in a sense, I needed more and deserve way more than what was passed off.

A nigga wanted a family and a wife someday, and the woman I was growing to love really wasn't giving me nothing but drama and drainage. She drained me of my energy, no matter how many times I tried to get her off the snow. She was more so interested in getting fucked and spending money, and those were things I no longer found exciting. Growth was a word I didn't want to take advantage of. When the Most High gave you chance after chance to do better, the right thing to do was get it right that second chance. What was the purpose of being successful if you didn't have anyone to share it with? It was pointless.

My phone began ringing. Looking at the screen, it was an unknown number. Everybody knew not to hit my cell from restricted numbers. I didn't even play like that, and it was rare it ever happened for real. If anyone called me unknown, I was bound to curse their ass out. For the second time, my phone rang.

I automatically got annoyed by the thought of another grown ass person going out of their way to do bullshit. That shit was nothing more than childish. I was big on saying it with your chest, standing on all ten of your toes. So, fucking with me, you have to say what you mean and mean what you say. It was the Taurus in me; a lot of people say that we were stubborn and bullheaded but, in reality, we just didn't fuck with the bullshit people tossed our way.

Taking a deep breath before answering the phone as it repeatedly rung, I prepared myself for what was next. Usually, when people called unknown, it was drama coming right after. My patience was far too thin to deal with any form of childishness.

"Hello?" I answered, slightly agitated. The other line was completely silent, and that was the shit that pissed me off. I rolled my eyes and hung up instantly. Soon as I sat my phone down, it lit up again. It was funny when people played games like this with me; my wrath was going to be felt. How do motherfuckers have so much time on their hands to do all of this shit? Pockets had to be on bum status. Answering the phone, I just knew Mocha's ass was being childish as fuck. Something was just telling me it was her ass.

"Aye, whoever the fuck this is calling my phone is childish as fuck! I'm gone ask you this just one time… stop playing on my line!" I snapped before hanging up. A response was something I didn't care for, especially when people were on some weirdo shit.

My phone was specifically for family and friends. People that were close to me and, occasionally, I would give it to a bitch or two, but it was rare. Mocha was really the only person that would bang this line. That's how I knew it was her ass playing and shit.

Today was a chill ass day; I wanted to go out and get some fresh air. The club was lit as hell last night, and the weekend definitely didn't owe me nothing. My mind felt like it needed some self-care, so I decided to get ready to hit the mall. After taking a nice hot and steamy shower, I dressed myself in a True Religion sweatsuit and a pair of coke white Air Force 1's. I slid on my Rolex, Louis Vuitton backpack, and grabbed the keys to my G-Wagon before heading out. Stonestown mall was calling my name.

Being raised by a single mom and going through struggles made me hungry. When I started hustling, it was because kids would pick on me for not having the latest Jordans. So, when the money began rolling in so quickly, I made sure everything that was on my wish list was purchased. Shit, I live a luxurious lifestyle and I was humble about it. It took me a good twenty minutes to make it to San Francisco.

The city was crowded and, of course, parking sucked. Once I found a spot, I locked my car and headed to the entry. It was the holiday season, so malls were usually overly crowded around this time. I didn't mind though; every once in a while, I'd pay for someone's stuff if we were in the same store. It was me paying it forward and giving back to someone in my own little way. There was no reason for me to not give back; my heart wasn't entirely frozen. My thuggish ways didn't take my heart away and the menace that lived inside me was there. I was just as human as anybody else was and I received judgment from each and every angle.

I walked around the mall hitting each and every store that caught my eye. Being a sneaker head was damn near an addiction, Footlocker was my top tier favorite store. You could never go wrong with some fresh ass kicks. Soon as I walked in the store, a female's eyes were glued to me. I chuckled to myself silently as I noticed that she was sitting with her man as he tried on shoes. Females were reckless; they didn't really give a fuck about shit when a nigga like me stepped through. I could tell she was getting a little choosy because her energy switched up and her man noticed. Little did she know, I wasn't checking for her.

"Do you got these in a size twelve?" I questioned one of the cashiers.

"Let me go to the back and check," the young boy replied

before walking off. I continued looking at the other pair of sneakers hanging from the wall.

No later than five minutes later, the store clerk came with a shoe box in hand. The chick was still staring me down and, when her nigga noticed, all hell broke loose.

"Is there a reason why you making eye contact with my bitch, bruh?" The dude snapped while walking towards me.

"Is there a reason why your bitch keep looking at me? You should be askin' shorty why she looking my way." I smirked.

There was absolutely no way possible I would be checking the next man over a female. It was clear as day he was frustrated and wanted to direct that shit my way, but I wasn't the one to talk. Shoot first and ask questions later was my motto.

"Who the fuck is you calling a bitch, nigga?" He questioned, pushing up on me.

"Nigga, now, I'm callin' you a bitch... bitch," I answered, clutching what I had on my waistband. I didn't care about anyone who witnessed; I had a lawyer and bail money.

"Yeah, aight nigga, don't let me see you outside this motherfucker," he threatened.

"I ain't scared brah," I chuckled.

"Bet nigga," he responded, snatching his bitch out the store.

Niggas were delusional. I never fonked with any nigga over a bitch. Women came and went, and I wasn't pressed over any woman. I couldn't help but laugh because be for real. After paying for my shoes, I decided to hit the food court. A nigga be hungry as hell after shopping, and Popeye's was sounding really good at this point.

The lines weren't too long; seeing the people with their kids warmed my heart. The reason why the holidays were special was because of families coming together. A familiar face caught my attention; her beauty was nothing but enticing. Ice's body was banging in street clothes. She was looking like a whole ass meal, fuck a snack. It was no way I was passing shorty up this time around. She ain't notice me though, which was perfect. Walking over to where she stood, I noticed a little girl with her.

"Wassup with you, love?" I questioned, as her eyes met mine.

"Umm, hello," she responded. She looked nervous as hell, and I had no reason as to why.

"Nice seeing yo beautiful self outside of work," I complimented, watching her smile slightly.

"I usually don't discuss work when I'm dealing with my personal life," she hinted, looking over at the child.

"Who may this little lady be?" I questioned, smiling at her.

"This is my daughter… Kiara," she answered.

"Hi Kiara," I greeted.

"Hi." She smiled hiding behind her mom's leg. Ice's genes were definitely strong as hell. Her daughter was a replica of her; she had copied Ice's entire face and that there was beauty.

"We were just grabbing lunch," she said.

"Shit, I was too. How about we eat together?" I suggested.

"Umm, sure… we were actually going for pizza," she replied.

"My treat," I insisted. She smiled, and we headed over to the Pizzeria.

"Icelynn." She smiled, holding out her hand for me to shake. Icelynn fit her vibe; she was stone cold and literally the baddest female I ever met. Nobody was fucking with her; she was everything.

"Frost," I responded. She looked at me like I was crazy. People never believed me when I told them that my government name was Frost.

"That's your real name or your street name?" She questioned.

"My street name Snowman, baby, and my real name Frost," I answered.

"Snowman huh? Why they call you that?" She pried.

"Because I'm the coldest nigga in the city… why they call you Ice?" I questioned back.

"Because I'm the coldest female with the pole work," she answered nonchalantly.

"Is that right?" I asked, smirking at her.

"That's right," she responded.

MOCHA

THE AFTER HOURS

Tonight was my first night back at the club. It was lit as fuck, and I just knew the bag was in the building. My life had been spiraling out of control and, since Frost stopped fucking with me, I'd been super high out of my mind. Him breaking it off with me really fucked my head up. I wasn't ready to let him go, but I also wasn't ready to let the coke go either. The music was booming and the drinks were coming; I was lit.

"Wassup Mami?" Plush greeted. She was one of my closest friends and the only one I had in this club. I ain't trust none of these bitches and I had a valid reason as to why I didn't.

"What's good? I see this shit packed out!" I replied.

"It is lit as fuck. Ever since that new girl came, niggas been lining up to get in," she answered.

"What new girl?" I questioned, raising my eyebrow. It had been a minute since some new bitches walked in here. I was the club OG but, lately, dancing hadn't even been on mind.

"You ain't peeped the Instagram stripper blogs?" Plush questioned.

"Nah, I ain't been on the net like that," I answered.

She pulled out her phone and scrolled for a second, then showed me a video on the Bay Areas Strippers tea page. It was a female dancing, which I assumed was Ice. She was beautiful and her body was giving natural. She was popping her shit in the video and doing her big one, I could admit, but she wasn't me.

Shorty had some moves though, and I could see her ambition in the way she moved. I could tell she had a passion for dancing by that alone. I was slightly impressed. If a bitch wanted my spot, she had to work for it. That was facts proven. I didn't make it easy on the girls in this club; they all had to work for their slot. Emerald, the club owner, would usually run the females by me before hiring them, and I'd be the one to train them on pole tricks and stripper etiquette. Even if I didn't show up, he'd call me and let me know he vibes.

"Who trained her?" I questioned, turning away from the screen and opening my locker.

"Nobody, she came in here ready. They said Emerald hired her on sight," Plush answered.

For some reason, that truly irritated me. This fat fuck clearly didn't give a fuck about my position in this club. I was the bottom bitch and everybody knew it.

"Is that right?" I questioned, silently chuckling to myself.

"Girl, yes. I'm about to get ready… my regular is requesting me," Plush answered before walking back out.

I definitely had a bone to pick with Emerald's fat ass. It was no secret that I'd held this club down for many years and earned the title as the bottom bitch. When Emerald lost every dime and couldn't pay to keep this club running during the pandemic, I made this ass shake hard as hell for seven days earning the funds to keep this club open for each bitch that needed a job. So, for Emerald to be going over my head when it came to the new bitches in the club, I was over it. There was no way possible he even thought this shit was okay. I had a weird ass feeling that this girl would run me out of my spot, and that was something that I wouldn't allow. I didn't give a fuck how talented a bitch was; she wasn't me and could never be. I didn't care how bitter shit may sound.

Slamming the locker door, I made my way up the stairs to his office. I really didn't give a damn about the door being closed. Pushing past the security guards, I entered the room with nothing but steam blowing from head. The security guards began to act as if they were suddenly doing their job after they had already let me bypass them. Kandy was between Emerald's legs sucking his funky little dick as if it was ring pop or some shit.

She instantly hopped up and ran right out of his office. My energy was definitely felt in that motherfucka. It was a matter of time before it really went up. He just sat his fat, musky, bald, one gold tooth having ass in that damn chair looking at me like I was crazy. The stupid motherfucker didn't have the decency to put his little beef stick away. I was disgusted and ready to speak my mind.

"So, we got new bitches in this piece of shit and you ain't run it against me? That's what we doing now, E?" I questioned, folding my arms.

"Mocha, first off, don't be coming into my office acting like I owe you something... you don't run shit in here," he spat.

"I have a position in this mothafucka and we made an agreement!" I replied as I became more livid than before coming in this office.

"Enlighten me," he smirked.

"I helped you with this club, I brought in every bitch that is here today... I trained them all and taught them the game," I said. "I am the bottom bitch, period." I added. He just stood there looking at me as if I simply didn't have any words coming out of my mouth.

"You letting the bottom bitch title get to your coked out ass head... you've been awol and have the nerve to come in here tripping on me," he responded.

Instead of responding, I remained silent; it was really nothing to say. He knew what the fuck we had planned and he took advantage of that, allowing someone else walk right on in. I ain't have time for shit like that, and he knew it would bother me.

"I'll tell you what sweetheart; you can either get down here and finish sucking this dick or get the fuck out and make some money… the choice is yours, so you better start thinking before I have those buff ass niggas embarrass you and carry you he fuck out of here." He smiled.

I was unsure why he thought that little shrimp dick of his would ever enter my mouth. Not even in his wildest dreams would my lips wrap around that thing; he was crazy out his mind. I did a lot of shit, but getting on my knees for Emerald was wild. Kandy wasn't the only female who did that nasty shit.

Most of the girls gave a little pussy to Emerald just because he was their boss and made them false ass promises. Because he owned this club, the delusion was at an all-time high; the dancers thought that they hit the jackpot fucking with his ass. Nobody knew this club was falling into pieces because as a real woman, I'd never throw motherfuckas that helped me under the bus. When I was just seventeen, Emerald gave me a job here doing the girls' hair. Because I was so young, dancing was out the window for me until my eighteenth birthday. Once my birthday came, the club became my full-time job and, eventually, Mocha was the most popular and requested dancer in this club.

He knew that, without me, wouldn't shit be afloat. I was determined to show out tonight; there was something to prove. I had to get to this bag because I was the bag. Sometimes, you just had to show a nigga better than you could tell them. Once I made it back to the locker room, my eyes instantly were laid on the new girl. She was pretty in person and the body was cool. I didn't care to introduce myself though. My mind was on the prize and getting the most money was the main goal. Showing Emerald I was really her was now the energy going forward. Being ducked off and under Frosty ain't do shit besides make me fall off of my game.

I slid on my fishnets along with a sparkly silver bra and thong set. The glow and the dark heels gave me a galactic look. I was definitely feeling the look as I wore my hair in two bun ponytails. My face was in full glam; I made sure Zoey beat my face to the gods. Tonight, I wasn't playing. Taking two shots of the Vodka, I headed straight to the stage. The music was booming as *Drip* by Capolow played. I began doing my dance leading up to a few tricks. After shaking, clapping, and moving my ass all over the stage, I began working the pole. The money was on the floor as the money flew from the air onto the stage. I began to light my heels on fire, allowing the crowd to go wild as I did a little spin upside down on the pole. I then clacked my heels together and came down on a handstand still going crazy. If doing your big one was a person, it was me. Once the song was over, I motioned to security to sweep my money off of the floor.

If they didn't know I was the baddest bitch, they fasho did now. Don't underestimate a Leo; whatever one did, I could do even better. I was the goat and everyone knew it. The euphoric feeling was better than the cocaine. Hearing the crowd go wild for me was priceless and gave me the high I needed.

When I made it to the dressing room to change my attire, Ice was finishing up her look. She wore a powder pink thong with nipple coverings to match; she wore powder pink heels to match. The girl cleaned up well, but she still wasn't fucking with me. I waited a couple of minutes before going out to the bar. I wanted another drink and also to be nosy and watch how the new girl worked. When I made it to the bar, Ice was on stage dancing to *Bag Long* by Dirty Dan.

"Long time no see," Trixie greeted.

"I know right? How you been girl?" I questioned loudly over the music.

"I been good girl…what are you drinking?" Trixie questioned.

"Can I get two shots of vodka with red bull," I replied as I watched Ice dance. She worked the pole like it was a canvas and she was the brush. Her style was completely different from mine. While I was more of a twerk dancer, she was more sensual and alluring.

"Coming right up!" she responded.

I watched as she poured the shot of vodka into the shot glasses. Once she sat them in front of me, I tossed them both back as the burning sensation filled my chest.

"Damn girl, you okay?" she asked.

I nodded my head and asked for another shot. Once she filled me up, I tossed them back and headed back to the dressing room. Fonzo, the security guard, gave me two money bags. They were filled to the brim.

My body was feinin' for some coke; I hadn't had a bump of cocaine in hours. It was still early and a matter of time before it was time for me to get my ass the hell out this club. My nerves were bothered and Emerald wasn't getting a tip out today. I didn't feel the need to give him shit. His fat funky ass had no right to talk to me the way he did after everything that I'd done for his ass.

I could show a motherfucker better than I could tell him though. Ice walked her happy ass in the locker room with four bags. Everyone was praising her when, in all honestly, I didn't see the hype. Yes, she was a beautiful woman and she had talent, that was something I could agree on, but the hype was crazy to me. She was just another bitch in the club like the rest of us. She was ordinary and that's just what it was. I slid my sweatpants on and a hoodie when Plush approached me with a confused ass look on my face.

"Why you leaving? You just got here," she questioned.

"I did what I needed to do; it's time to go," I answered, shoving the garbage bag inside of my duffel. I was tired any ways and the club wasn't giving me the respect that I needed.

"Girl, you're corny. We barely fucking see you around anymore," Plush replied. She was right; nobody had been seeing me in a while. I been too busy and preoccupied traveling with Frost's ass and living life with him. Now that he cut me off completely, I was trying to build myself up to get back to my old self. Healing from someone that you genuinely loved was hard.

I blamed myself often for Frost cutting me off though. He had put up with my shit for a long time and tried to support me and get my ass off the coke. However, I just didn't have the desire to quit. What I craved was his love more than anything, but I couldn't stay away from the drugs at all. It became an addiction and I used that shit to mask how I felt. Stripping was a hard ass job and coming into an environment like that, the best thing to do was either drink all night or numb yourself up with whatever drug that was out there. I couldn't help that it became the norm for me. Everything was so regular due to the fact my lifestyle was spinning so fast. This game was something that I badly wanted out of but, the money was coming so quick, I couldn't walk away from it. Money being the root to all evil had to be a factual saying. The money had turned me into a demon.

"Girl, I'll hit you later," I responded, walking past her. I went out the building side door and exited the club. Once I made it inside of my car, I poured the cocaine on my right hand and snorted a little over a bump. Tossing my head back, allowing the powdering substance to take over my body, I wiped my nose before closing the small baggy. Sitting there stuck in my thoughts, Frost's car pulled into the parking lot. Before I could bounce out and check the nigga, I saw this bitch Ice walking out of the building straight towards him. My heart instantly sunk in. I couldn't stand to see this nigga love somebody, especially this bitch.

I felt a mixture of jealousy and rage over come me. Instead of bouncing out the car and acting crazy as hell, I decided to respectfully pull off. How the fuck did he even meet this girl was the question circulating throughout my mind? Was she the reason he had been acting funny towards me? He had been so distant and pushing me away from him. As the tears streamed down my face, I tried to shake the thoughts, but my reality had set in. I really lost my man because I couldn't get it together.

LATER THAT NIGHT...

I spent an hour scrolling through this girl's page and comparing myself to her. I felt super insecure at the moment and that feeling was entirely fucked up. I had one thought on my mind and that was possibly breaking everything in that nigga's house and demanding answers. I picked up my phone, instantly calling my best friend. It was so funny to me that bitches in the club being buddy buddy with a hoe that was clearly fucking with my man.

The way he held her in his arms was a way that he had never held me. That shit hurt and made me feel some type of way entirely. The closure was needed because we had a good thing going and now, all of the sudden, we didn't have that vibe anymore. I didn't think he'd give up on me or our bond like that, yet he did. Was it my fault?

"Hello?" Plush answered.

"Hey, are you busy?" I questioned, hoping she would say no. I desperately needed a friend to call on and a shoulder to cry on.

"I'm about to go do a private event, why, what's wrong?" she responded.

"Nothing, never mind. Be careful boo, love you," I

answered and, before she could get a word out, I hung up. I was pretty sure bitches knew what was up.

I was starting to feel like all my little bonds and friendships were slowing falling apart, and I was noticing that shit. It was difficult to deal with in the beginning when Frost cut me off. Now, it's settling with me that he was serious when he told me that he didn't want to be with me anymore. My heart was feeling very weak and broken. Closing out every open app on my phone, I turned it off and tossed it across the room. The last thing I wanted to do was stalk this bitch social media and feel sad over a nigga. My happy place was calling my name, the *snow*.

ICELYNN

Last night was a complete vibe. I made so much fucking money last night, it was unbelievable. It felt amazing to have money flowing in my household and being able to take care of my daughter without struggling. Investing was on my mind heavy as hell, and stripping was something that I didn't plan on doing forever; it was only for the time being.

The goal was to create wealth that could go down to my daughter in the future. She was deserving of at least a mother who did what they could for the sake of her child. I was willing to give up my entire life to make sure my daughter didn't have to worry about a thing.

I grew up seeing all type of shit a mother shouldn't want

her kid to be exposed to. I made sure that no matter what, Kiara didn't have to experience any of that. My mother and her drug habit was insane. She chose some shit over me, allowing her first born daughter to get caught up in the system. That shit wasn't right at all and, in my opinion, I was failed the moment she gave birth to me.

It was rather fucked up that this was my life and I didn't have not one family member in sight. My daughter always asked me if she had a grandma from my side and the answer was always the same. Building my own family was something I craved and didn't receive but, eventually, it'd come.

I scrolled through my Instagram feed; it was crazy how my following was going up overnight. The thought of doing private parties crossed my mind, but I also thought about a movie called *The Players Club*. Ronnie always had females in sticky situations and the way she set Ebony up always broke my fucking heart. It was no way possible that I ever wanted that type of energy for myself. I didn't need anyone trying to play with me or trying to place me in harmful situations when I had a whole daughter to live for.

My phone began ringing, snapping me right out of my thoughts. It was none other than Frost. We'd been talking over time and getting to know one another. Our connection was crazy and we shared an amazing vibe. I couldn't wait to see where things could possibly go with him.

"Hello?" I answered with a big ass smile planted across my face.

"Wassup my baby?" he questioned. His deep ass voice sent chills through my body, making my pussy wet instantly.

Fat ma was definitely purring at the sight of the man and the sound of his voice.

"Not much, I was just thinking about future goals and plans," I answered.

"I want to learn more about your goals and plans. That shit is attractive," he responded, making me blush again.

"I have a child, shit. I want more for her, so it's important to want more for myself," I truthfully said.

"Maybe I can help you accomplish those goals… are you busy right now?" Frost questioned.

"Not really, I was just about to go tree shopping while Kiara is with her grandmother," I answered.

"Can I go with you?" He questioned.

Tree shopping together was a surprise for me. I wasn't expecting that shit from nobody. It was sweet though. It was the gesture I appreciated the most, especially coming from a man like him. "Sure, I'd actually love that. How about I pick you up in the next hour?" I questioned.

"Picking me up is crazy, you can be ready in an hour though. I'll swoop you," he chuckled.

"Aw, you don't want to be the passenger prince?" I questioned.

"Nah, baby, but you can be my passenger princess," he responded.

I couldn't help but laugh at his ass because he was truly a funny ass nigga. "Whatever, see you in a little bit Frost," I responded with a chuckle as I hung the phone up.

Heading upstairs to lay out my outfit, I decided on putting on a pair of black leggings, a crop hoodie, and a pair of classic Vans. The look was giving chilled and laid back. I put my hair into a high ponytail and laid my edges down in perfection. It was always a cute and simple day for me when I had errands to run.

Once I was satisfied with my overall look, I went downstairs to wait on Frost. My phone began ringing and I noticed it was my best friend, Cristal. I missed her ass so much. I met Cristal when we were teenagers; running away from group homes was a trauma bond we shared. We looked out for one another and that's how we ended up locked in. We were so close that nothing else mattered. We were tight like sisters, and that was something no one could take away from us. If she was swinging, know that I was and vice versa.

"Hey boo!" she spoke excitedly through the phone.

"Hey best, what you doing?" I questioned.

"Not much mamas, I'm just heading out," she answered.

"Where are you going?" I meddled. It had been a while since we had a girls' night and I so badly wanted to spend some girly time with my best friend. Since I'd been at the club, we hadn't had much time with each other.

"I'm going to have a little beauty day and get some dick," she chuckled.

"Some dick? From who?" I questioned, meddling in her business.

"From the nigga of my dreams, bitch! When you gonna find you one?" Cristal joked.

"Actually, I think I've found him," I responded.

I had to truthfully admit that I was feeling Frost. He was a sweetheart but also his dominance made me want him more.

Right now, I was now in my softest girl era and I needed to be with someone who made me feel safe and secure. I couldn't help but enjoy this part of my life. The love I wanted would soon come to me and, hopefully, it was with Frost.

"Whom are you speaking of?" My best friend meddled. She wanted to be in my business so bad.

"This nigga I met at the club," I answered with a smile plastered across my face. The thought of him made me feel super gushy and happy inside. Those feelings were something that I hadn't had in a long time.

"I know you ain't meet no nigga at that damn club trying to turn him into a husband," she replied.

"Girl, nobody said nothing about no husband, but he fasho a cool nigga and I like him so far," I responded.

"Well, then, bitch… who is it?" She questioned.

"This nigga named Frost, he from around the way," I answered.

"Oh, shit bitch!" She blurted.

I was super curious as to why she reacted that way. I was hoping that she wasn't fucking with the same nigga I was up on. Cutting off my new favorite nigga was insane. "Don't tell me that my guy is your guy." I sighed.

"Not my guy! But he is definitely somebody's nigga. This girl named Mocha that works at the club… I'm gone send you a pic of her," she responded.

"Okay, I guess," I replied. Before I knew it, my phone was notifying me that I had an Instagram direct message. Before I could enlarge the picture, I noticed that it was the girl from the club last night.

"What's her name?" I questioned, clicking on the girl's page.

"It's Mocha, she from around the way," she answered.

After scrolling through the girl's page for a couple of minutes, I learned so much about her. She had no children, was at one point the top-notch dancer at the club, and she indeed was involved with Frost. The highlights on her page were showing nothing but fly ass trips they took together.

If he had a girlfriend, why would he ever pursue me? This shit was throwing me off entirely, and I didn't like it at all. He wasn't my man, but he definitely had potential to be. The vibe that he was giving was definitely hinting around a relationship tip. We had a great start off and, to me, hiding shit was the biggest throw off a nigga had to offer. I ain't have any time for that shit. A part of me wanted to question him about it, but the other half mainly wanted him to come to me first. I didn't want any unnecessary drama, especially over a man I just met. It wasn't nowhere worth it to me.

I could only give him the chance to come to me with the truth. If he was not willing to do that much, then maybe he wasn't the right man for me and, if that was so, then it was all good. My doorbell began ringing. Looking at the ring camera from my phone, it was Frost. I dismissed the conversation with my best friend.

Once she was off the phone, I walked to the front door to let Frost inside. The attitude I had was semi through the roof and I didn't want him to even know that the relationship he had or had with Mocha was throwing me off. After thinking about everything and convincing myself to let it go, I eventually did. There was no way that his past would interfere with what we were building. I enjoyed the moments I'd spent with him, even though it hadn't been many moments shared. I was interested in having more time built with him. Approaching the door to open it for Frost, I took a deep breath, trying to wash away the negative thoughts that I had and the slight feelings that were super noticeable as well.

"Wassup beautiful?" He greeted me.

"Hi… I'm ready, let me grab my purse," I responded while walking away, ignoring the fact that he was trying to embrace me with a hug. My energy was felt and it was stronger than a motherfucker.

After grabbing everything that I needed and setting my home alarm, I thought about confronting him for multiple reason. One, being, why would you bother me when you know that you have a woman in your life? The other reason why I wanted to confront him was because he had been in my face constantly, making me feel like I was something that he wanted. Being a single mother, my daughter and I was a packaged deal. I didn't allow niggas around me or her and to have Frost around was new. Temporary shit was not in my deck of cards and my hopes were that he knew that.

"How you feeling ma?" Frost questioned, as I buckled my seat belt.

"I'm cool," I responded nonchalantly, turning my attention back to my phone. My headphones were in as I listened to this podcast on YouTube. Talking to Frost wasn't giving the vibes and energy that I wanted and needed in this moment.

My irritation was fresh and I held back how I really felt to avoid confrontation.

"Why you so dry with me?" He questioned before pulling out of the driveway.

"I'm not," I lied.

"Nah, you is and you know that you are," he responded.

"Can we go?" I questioned. Turning my feelings off was something I did when I realized how certain motherfuckers got down. He hid something from me and didn't come forward about it off top, and that was red flag in my defense.

"Stop playing with me, we not going nowhere until you start talking. That pouting and attitude shit not going to work with me," Frost answered.

"Why the fuck you ain't tell me that you had a girlfriend? Why the fuck you in my face and coming into my world knowing you got baggage?" I interrogated. Since he wanted me to say something, I was saying it.

"Woah, what is you on for real?" He questioned in confusion.

"I'm on what you on baby, so what the fuck is good?" I replied. The fact that he looked hella confused was really sending me to an uproar.

"I don't have a girlfriend Icelynn, haven't had a girlfriend in years for real." Frost sighed.

Those pictures in that girl's highlights looked real couple like and the highlights dated back to forty-two weeks ago and stopped about a week ago. "Lying to me ain't gone get you anywhere, no cap love," I responded. This little conversation wasn't going anywhere.

"You cuff every little stripper huh? You got a thing for private dancers?" I questioned in laughter. I was over this shit already, unbuckling the seat belt and hopping out the car heading to my front door.

I stuck my key in my front door and twisted the knob, as Frost followed behind me. Arguing wasn't something I was interested in doing. It wasn't anything to really talk about when he was clearly on some bullshit. All he had to do was be real about it and maybe I'd respect that shit and give him a fair chance. Niggas didn't realize that all they really had to do was be real and being real was the realist shit anyone could do, especially when it had something to do with my feelings or shit they hiding.

"Walking into my house uninvited is crazy Frost, what do you want? You can't even be real," I chuckled, kicking my shoes off.

"Nah, I told you what's up Icelynn. I'm a real nigga first, I ain't fucking with nobody right now... I'm trying to pursue you and only you," he responded, grabbing me by the waist. "That girl was never my girlfriend, we were just bonding without a title. We were fucking around, and she started doing trifling shit that made me fall back off of her. I ain't been fucking with her and I don't want her... I'm on you and I'm focused on just you," he explained.

He looked me dead in my eyes, and that look he gave me made my ass weak as hell. I wanted to be mad at him so bad, but the way this nigga had my kitty purring, being mad wasn't even a part of the plans. I felt secure in his words but I wasn't going to allow anyone else to come into my world and hurt me.

"Don't lie to me," I replied.

"I'm not lying to you, ma. Let my actions show you," he said, pulling me closer to him. He had me like puddy in his hands, all soft and shit.

His lips pressed against mine as our tongues wrestled. Right then, I signed a deal with death row and I wasn't even going to back out of it. As his hands cuffed both of my ass cheeks, he lifted me up, allowing me to wrap both legs around his waist. Our lips locked for a solid two minutes before he carried me up the stairs to my bedroom. Having sex wasn't my plans, but the way I was drenched underneath this thong was crazy.

"You sure this is what you want?" He questioned, lying me on the bed. I didn't even have the words; I simply nodded my head, giving him the green light to take control of my body.

As he pulled his clothes off, I did the same. It had been a good minute since I had some sexual attention; this man didn't know that he was in for a treat. I couldn't help but stare at the big ass bulge in his drawers. Frost grabbed me by my legs and pulled me to the edge of the bed before pulling my panties off. My freshly waxed and wet pussy was exposed to him, and his eyes lit up like a kid in the candy store. Frost brought his face between my thighs and instantly began feasting on me as if I was the last supper.

His tongue was making me feel superior as he sucked on my clit and fingered me in a nice pace. I couldn't help but let out soft moans as my legs began to tremble and shake. He replaced his two fingers with his tongue and, instantly, I came all over his face. I laid there gasping, as he propped himself between my legs and rubbed the tip of his dick on my juice box, making me beg for it. Teasing me was crazy. I grabbed his hard nine and inserted it right inside of me, causing us both to moan. He felt amazing inside of me, and I could tell that he enjoyed being inside of my honeypot.

"Damn Mami," he moaned, stroking inside of me. His manly moans turned me on even more. I just wanted to get off by pleasing him. He pulled his dick out of my pussy and instructed me to get on all fours. I did exactly as instructed, allowing my arch to show.

He gripped my ass with both hands and thrusted in me roughly. The pain turned into instant pleasure as I gasped for air. With every stroke, I felt euphoric. His dick had me floating on a cloud that I didn't want to come up off of. He smacked my ass, as I threw it back. I began to cream all over his dick, causing him to curse and pick up his pace.

"This pussy so fucking good, damn!" He complimented, pulling by my hips.

I loved when a nigga told me how good my pussy was, it made me wanna go crazier. Before he could cum, I pulled his manhood out of me and began sucking my juices off. I pushed his meat to the back of my throat and began slurping him up like crazy. The joy of watching his eyes roll to the back of his head made me wetter. He began playing with my pussy while I allowed him to stroke my mouth. If you googled throat goat, I'd more than likely pop up. Rubbing my tongue on the head of his dick, I instantly start rubbing his balls, easing every inch of him to the back of my throat.

"Mmmm…" I moaned.

"Damn, like just that," he groaned.

I was hardheaded and listening wasn't something I did well. I shoved his balls in my mouth and hummed a little, allowing the vibration of my mouth to make him cum all over my face.

I didn't mind getting slutty for a nigga that was being real with me and treated me right. I stuck my tongue out, allowing the rest of his nut to seep to the back of my throat before swallowing. For the rest of the evening, I allowed him to slut me out. This nigga created a demon and, over him, it was demon time.

FROSTY

I couldn't help but feel amazing after the bomb ass sex I had with Icelynn. Not only was she a dope ass woman, but her pussy was addictive. Her little attitude told me alone she had some good coochie on her but, after today, I already knew wassup. The fact that this bitch Mocha was still posting me on her social media was crazy. We had nothing more to discuss or talk about. She was delusional as hell. Shorty chose her side when she started playing with the snow.

I hated that for her; you snooze on a good nigga, you lose. I was definitely feeling Ice though. She was every bit of woman I needed. She was everything without trying too hard and our vibe was naturally there. She gained a whole new ounce of respect from me. I adored how great of a mother she was. The way she kept my head straight in the short amount of time of knowing her made me feel great.

Looking over at how peaceful she slept, I kissed her forehead softly and slid out the bed. My phone was ringing back-to-back and I had no clue whom it might've been. I was glad my shit was silenced though because the last thing I needed was more attitude from Icelynn. Grabbing my phone off the nightstand, I headed downstairs to the kitchen to pour me a glass of juice. My phone lit up, indicating a call was coming through from an unknown number. I had no clue who the fuck it was and, in my head, the hopes of it not being Mocha was high.

"Who this?" I answered in a stern tone. I needed niggas to know I wasn't in the mood for bullshit.

"This Ceddy, our spot got ran down on!" Cederick spoke.

"Nigga, what? You just now calling me?" I snapped. Taking a loss in my business was unacceptable; that was a whole pot of bullshit I didn't have time for.

"We've been blowing you up for the last three hours bruh. Yo ass ain't answering my nigga, that ain't our fault… this shit ain't on us!" He snapped back.

"Watch your fucking tone! I'll be to the hood in a minute," I responded, hanging up the phone. I didn't know who the fuck these young niggas thought they were, but there was no way that he was talking to me.

"Babe? You good?" Icelynn questioned, walking into the kitchen. Her face was bare of no makeup and lashes, just pure beauty that calmed my nerves entirely.

"Nah ma, I'm not gone cap. I gotta go deal with some shit," I answered.

"I don't want you to go, but I understand babe," she pouted. Her little cute ass knew I'd rather be under her. However, when money was involved, I had had to get to it.

"I'm coming back mamas, I promise," I replied, pulling her into a tight hug. She held on to me tightly and I made sure I did the same.

"You better keep your fucking word or else." She sighed.

"You sending threats?" I asked, looking her in the eyes.

"Maybe." She smiled. Her ass was good at seducing me and going for another round didn't sound bad at all.

"I promise, I'm gone come back mamas," I assured her. We shared one last kiss before I got dressed and left her crib.

RICH CITY

The entire room was silent, didn't nobody have an answer for me. Losing money and getting my spots ran into wasn't something I wanted to go down. I needed direct answers and, if they weren't going to give me that, bodies were going to start dropping, even if they were men in my own crew. Someone knew something.

"Tell me who the fuck is responsible for my spot getting hit? I need answers now, not later, so get to fucking talking before a body get dropped," I spoke angrily.

"I ain't gone lie, word around town that nigga Dubbz

fucking with the suckas maybe he got us hit," Jrock said, breaking the silence.

"Nigga, I don't fuck with suckas! Fuck is you talking about?" Dubbz replied, clutching his gun.

"Dubbz, you playing in my face?" I questioned.

"Nah, bruh, I don't even play like that," Dubbz answered.

"Matter a fact, I did see you around the way with that nigga Smurf." I smirked. This nigga thought that I was stupid. He fasho been talking and it was an matter of time before he was swimming with the fishes.

"Man, I don't fuck with Smurf... you ain't seen me with that nigga," Dubbz replied.

"It's the fact that you standing in my face lying for me," I chuckled, pulling my forty caliber out and pressing the cold steel against his forehead. "Speak now or take it to the grave lil nigga!" I snapped.

"I don't hang with that ni-" he stuttered.

BOOM! BOOM!

I let off two shots into his body as it collapsed to the ground. It was gone be one cold ass winter if niggas thought that they were going to have one up on me. I wasn't having it, and the snake shit and lying in my face made it even worse for him because why would you even feel this comfortable doing weird shit in my face? I didn't have any answers for that and, even if he wasn't responsible for my spot getting ran through and robbed, he still lied in my face. That was enough to get popped, and I was making examples out of these niggas. Wasn't nobody going to disrespect me or play games. One do it, they were all going to do it and that I couldn't have.

At this point, I couldn't trust none of these niggas. I just lost ten keys of the purest Cuban coke these streets ever seen, along with fifty thousand in cash. Not only did I lose my bands, but I also lost my product. Nobody in this city had the balls to fuck with my snow, so whomever felt the need to play was going to suffer tremendously. When orders were given to these niggas, the only job that they had was to follow them. I didn't give a fuck about shit, but my count being right and my money adding up to what I needed it to be. My motto was peace and prosperity; having blood on my hands wasn't something I wanted but, if I needed to, then I would.

"Toss this nigga with the fishes and the next nigga to lie in my face and play getting popped up," I demanded before walking off.

I hurried my ass up so that I could make it back to my peace, Icelynn.

LATER THAT EVENING...

Pulling up to Icelynn's house, I sat out in the driveway for a little bit trying to blow off a little steam. Walking into her home with this angry energy wasn't something that I wanted to do. After a few minutes, I walked up to the door and rang the doorbell. A few minutes later, the door swung open. She had Keaira on her hip and appeared to had just woke up.

"Hey baby," she greeted, stepping aside, and letting me in.

I kissed her forehead, as Keaira was sleeping on her shoulder peacefully. "Sup ma?" I questioned, pulling my jacket off and hanging it on the coat rack.

"Let me go lay her down in her room real quick; she hadn't been feeling good at all today," Icelynn answered, walking towards the stairs.

I watched her walk up, as her ass jiggled in the grey leggings she had on. I made myself comfortable on the couch and grabbed the remote control from the glass coffee table. I didn't really watch too much TV but, every once in a while, I'd tune into the news just to see what the hell was going on in the world around me. The streets talked enough for me to get the scoop, but checking the stations out gave me a little insight on some things. Moments later, Icelynn came back down the stairs yawning.

"What's up babe? You okay?" She questioned.

"I'm stressed, I'll be alright though," I answered.

"What's going on? Talk to me," she poked again.

Talking about this shit really wasn't going to make me feel better. Shutting her out completely wouldn't either though. "I ain't gone lie, one of my trap spots got hit and I lost a lot of money… this shit had to be a setup. Only people that work with me knew about this location." I sighed.

"Oh no, I'm sorry baby. You can't trust people these days… niggas be jealous and spiteful," she replied.

That was something that I already knew. Trusting people could land me in a whirl of trouble. Giving the wrong people my trust and trying to help everyone eat really bit me in the ass. "I already know, that's why I can't push no weight in that location. Somebody was either snaking me or watching me," I said, rubbing my hands across my face.

"You've got to switch up the routine and change locations," she suggested.

"That's extra work and possibly more bodies, especially if I can't get the territory I need to make it possible," I explained.

"Let me help you," she replied.

Those were some words that I really didn't expect to here, especially coming from her. "What you mean?" I questioned, raising an eyebrow.

"Let me move your product throughout the club... nobody is going to even know it's me, and I know the whole lay out and system. I can help you babe if you believe in me. You're not alone," she stated. I just said how trusting people could get you fucked over and I didn't want to kill Icelynn for fucking me over.

However, her idea wasn't bad at all. That's why I fucked with Icelynn. Not only was she beautiful and talented, but she was about her bag and she for sure just made me feel like she had my back. A get money bitch with good pussy and she hold her nigga down? That shit was every nigga's dream. As long as the loyalty was there and she didn't cross me, I'd make sure that she was taken care of and protected.

ICELYNN

I didn't know what I was getting myself into, but I knew that I wanted to be Frost's rider. I wanted to be the one he relied on and the one that had his back through thick and thin. My feelings for him were real. He made me feel shit that I didn't think that I'd ever feel. Not only was the dick good, but he was gentle with me and I felt safe in his presence. Selling drugs wasn't my forte; I was a scamming ass bitch but, if I did this shit right, it would all work out well.

The hoes in the club sold pussy for a living, a little drugs in that motherfucker wasn't going to hurt anyone. I trusted my man enough to know he'd look out for me, especially since I was doing him a solid. As secure as he made me feel, it was only right that he felt the same exact way that I did.

Although I wasn't fully prepared for what would come out of this, I mentally made myself ready. Frost taught me the ends and outs of the game. It was simple and easy, just like stripping. All I had to do was get about three bitches into the club that was ready to work and make money. I wasn't so sure if I could trust anyone inside the club, so forming my own team would be a better choice for me.

"You sure you wanna do this?" Frost questioned.

I wasn't sure, but I knew doing this wouldn't only put him in a good position but me as well. "Yeah," I responded.

"I got your back. I'm going to make sure you stay protected and we going to get to this bread, but I will not have you in this life if this isn't something you want to be doing for real," he explained.

"I'm grown baby, I got this. A whole plan in my head," I assured him. Once I had my team built, I'd be ready in no time. The more hands, the easier I could maneuver.

"Tomorrow night, I'm going to give you some soft snow to push at the club… I wanna see how much you get off before I let you in. I gotta see what you can do," he explained.

He didn't know what type of bitch he was dealing with. My name was Icelynn and I was the princess of Ice City. Having everything on lock came to me naturally. There was no way I would fuck it up, especially when I move more militant than niggas.

"Frost, I got this. I ain't no weak ass bitch, neither am I green… I got this, I got us," I responded.

"Say less," he replied as he pulled me on top of him. I was now straddling his lap as we were face to face, looking one another dead in the eyes.

"Getting money together is my love language, you know that?" he questioned.

"Quality time is mine," I answered, rubbing my fingers through his head full of locs. The butterflies in my stomach were floating around every time this man laid his eyes on me or even touched me. Shit, breathing the same air as him had me going wild.

"You get all of that. Time is of an essence and I don't have any to waste," he replied, holding me tightly in a hug.

"Be careful with me… I'm fragile," I admitted.

"As long as you got me, I got you," he assured.

THE AFTER HOURS….

It was another lit night at the club. This whole shit was packed out and it was nothing but money on the floor on each end. Frost was here to ensure that I was good while moving the cocaine through the club. I pretty much could tell by energy who was a powder head and who wasn't. Frost gave me exactly a zip of cocaine.

He wanted to see how I moved it and, by the looks of the upper level V.I.P. section, this shit was going to be sold in no time. I strutted my way to that section. I had the cocaine stashed in baggies hidden over my body in tuck spots like my breasts, pussy, and in my heels as well as taped underneath. I was determined to show my man how hard I fucked with him and also make extra cash for my daughter and me.

"Hey honey, are you looking for a good time?" I questioned the two white men that were hanging at the bar on the second floor.

"Hell, yea sweet cakes!" The fat stocky one answered, leading me over to the V.I.P. section.

I already knew what I was in for. The whole section was full of four white guys and two scrawny ass white girls. I didn't know who told them to come dance at this club, but, tonight, bitches had to dip up out of here. It was money calling my name and I wasn't letting nobody step on my toes.

"I'm sorry, this my section, y'all gotta step," I sassed, booting the two hoes out the mix. With no hesitation, they both dipped.

"Call Cream up here real quick," I told the security guard. Cream was the only girl in this club I felt could sit with me. She was a bad ass Dominican chick from New York. This was her second night in this club and my fourth. When I met her, she clung to me and we'd been dynamic since. I didn't know too much about her but, from what was observed, she was a complete vibe.

She had long jet-black hair, big beautiful doll eyes, and long natural lashes. She was a stallion standing at approximately 5'8 with a curvy ass body. She had a thick ass Spanish accent with a mixture of New York slang, making her sound foreign as hell. She was an exotic bitch, and I loved a bad bitch.

I entertained the men with some slight lap dancing, as

Cream approached the section. Once security let her in, that's when the real turn up began. These white folks were throwing money on us nonstop and tossed drinks back. One of the guys did a bump right in front of me and, just like that, I had the green light. He became my first knock of the night. A knock was a user, someone who bought drugs. It didn't matter if you were copping some dope or weed, you were looked at as a knock.

Tonight was the night for me. I moved around that club swiftly making my money. I wiggled my way to Frost, letting him know we were up fourteen hundred dollars off of the one zip he provided me with. While we were chopping it up, my favorite song came on and I began twerking on him. He pulled out his stacks from the duffel and began making it rain on me. All the money he was tossing in the air on me brought a lot of attention to our area.

"Aww shit, Ice and Frost cuttin' the fuck up y'all!" the DJ hollered over the music.

I smiled as everyone pulled out their cameras on flash mode, filming us. Once the cameras came out, we both started acting up and showing out. I loved how Frost matched my energy. He was such a boss ass nigga and it showed. He smacked my ass, as I made it clap something crazy. I blew a kiss to the camera and he snatched my ass up and kissed me, marking me as his territory in front of all the niggas in this building.

"Aww shit! It's lover's lane in this muhfucka!" the DJ boasted.

Just as I began to blush, Mocha was coming in our direction. If pissed off was a person, it was definitely her. She was livid and it showed.

"This what we doing? Kissing random bitches?" Mocha questioned Frost.

"Watch yo fucking mouth when you talking about my girl!" Frost snapped.

"Yo girl? Your dick was just in my mouth, now all of a sudden, she ya girl!" Mocha shouted over the music.

This bitch had five seconds to walk the fuck off before I whooped her ass and moved her ass out my way. "Listen bitch, I don't know what y'all had going on before, but that shit is over now," I chimed in.

"You don't even know Frost. You just start coming around, I been here," she responded.

The fact that she was trying me and not knowing me, Mocha was talking out the side of her neck like I wouldn't break it.

"You not about to keep sitting here disrespecting my female. We are not together Mashanti, get that shit through yo thick ass skull!" He snapped, pulling me away. That's how I knew he was mad because he rarely called me by my government name.

"Go get yo shit and let's go!" Frost demanded.

"I have to do my pay out first," I reminded him.

"You good, I already gave it to 'em. Just throw yo shit on and come on," he replied.

Without any further delay, I grabbed my money bags and slipped my clothing on before making my grand exit. All eyes were now focused on me, especially since the little scene between Mocha and Frost. He stamped and let everybody know I was his girl and, after the money I made with him, shit was gone be a nice little breeze. When I told Frost that I got us, I meant that shit whole heartedly.

MOCHA

The fact that this nigga completely humiliated me in front of this bitch and the entire club was crazy. When a new bitch felt the need to check me was even more wild. I didn't know who the fuck Ice was, but there was homework to be done on that bitch. She came out of nowhere and, all of a sudden, everyone just fucked with her.

The jealousy was flowing, I fell off and somebody else stepped in. That shit made me feel low. I took a bump to the nose and tossed my head back. The euphoric feeling took my name off of everything that I had on my mind. I left the club with the same trick that was dropping bags om Cream and

Ice. He had hella money and coke, so I took advantage of his time while I could.

"You ready for a good time?" Tyler smiled, walking towards the hotel bed as he unbuttoned his shirt.

"As long as we continue partying like this, I'm going to always have a good time," I answered.

"You are one beautiful girl, do you know that?" Tyler smirked.

The tone in his voice gave me an uneasy feeling, but the way I was floating on the drugs tuned my feelings out. I laid there smiling back at him before snorting another line. He was now standing right before me asshole naked, looking like a fucking raw piece of chicken legs. I ain't like that not one little bit. Fucking the white man sounded crazy to me, but I was down to do it anyways. I ain't never mind getting a little kinky here and there, especially when it came down to some money or drugs. Me being a fiend was impossible; having control over myself was something that was in me. My body knew when it had too much and when to slow down.

As Tyler got closer to me, reality set in. This man in my eyesight made me even more disgusted with myself than I was before. He sat on the bed right next to me and began touching my bare legs. My thoughts continued to tell him to stop, but the words weren't flowing out as fast as I wanted them to.

"I don't think I want to do this anymore," I began.

"What you mean? I already paid you... we're doing this alright!" Tyler snapped.

"I can give you back the money," I suggested, and the look on his eyes told me that he wasn't having it.

Before my feet could even hit the ground, he smacked me so hard, my body flew to the opposite side of the bed. He grabbed me by legs, pulled me down to the foot of the bed and straddled himself on top of me. As high as I was, his body weight was overpowering me. Screaming as loud as I could, I tried to wiggle myself out of Tyler's tight grasp, but he pulled a knife from under his pillow and held it to my throat. The fear pumping within me had me so shook to the point where just lying there became my best option. My brain went numb as he violated every inch of my body. He made sure that each hole went untouched. I laid in the puddle of blood, and he had the audacity to throw two hundred dollars at me.

Did I really just get raped? My mind wouldn't process nothing that was circulating through my mind. I laid there for three whole minutes before getting my ass up. My legs felt entirely stuck as my head spun. I limped to the wooden table that sat underneath the mounted TV, grabbing my purse. Pulling my phone out of my handbag, the first person I called was Frost. Although we got into it earlier at the club, I knew that he'd come to my rescue. Frost was all I ever had and the only nigga that I loved for real. Dialing his number in my phone, it rang straight to voicemail. I continued to call a few times, and he still didn't answer.

The thought that I had about he always would be here for me was pushed to the farthest part of my brain. It was now crystal clear that I obviously meant nothing to him. Hating it here was at an all-time high, and I could only blame myself because of my own actions. I hurried and put my clothes on and ran out of the motel doors. I couldn't take it anymore; so many emotions were built up inside of me.

———

I WOKE UP WITH A BANGING ASS HEADACHE IN AN UNFAMILIAR room, not knowing where I was and how I ended up here. My ears were ringing and my eyes were now fully opened. The walls of the room were painted a burnt orange color and there were some art portraits hanging from the walls. The furniture around me looked very old and dingy. I knew for a fact that this wasn't any place I'd volunteered to come to. My anxiety instantly got triggered as I began having flashbacks of what went down with the white boy, Tyler.

"Someone's awake," the unfamiliar voice said, interrupting me from my thoughts. My thoughts were extremely negative. I was thankful to be snapped from them. Reliving something so traumatizing was a wall I didn't care to bump into.

"DO I KNOW YOU?" I QUESTIONED AS MY EYES MET THE FACE OF an older black woman. She stood at five foot three and had her hair parted down the middle in two curly poof ball ponytails. She was very skinny but appeared to be athletic. She had a nice-looking body for an elder. Her caramel skin was full of freckles and she had hazel-colored eyes.

"No, you don't. You was passed out on the sidewalk on the side of the road. I wanted to take you to the hospital and leave you there, but my good heart wouldn't let me do that," she explained, using a very soft-spoken tone.

"On the side of the road?" I questioned in confusion. The only thing I remembered was running outside the room.

"That's right, on the side of 580 in the rain," she answered. How the fuck did I even end up there was the real question that I needed answers to.

"I don't remember any of this happening," I responded.

"Sweetheart, maybe we should get you to a hospital. You don't look too good," she replied.

"No, thank you. Can you just call my friend for me please? I'll have someone pick me up," I responded. I prayed silently to myself that Frost answered his line this time.

"I'm going to only ask you this one time… do you need to go to the hospital?" She questioned.

"No ma'am," I replied. Denying medical attention was something that I knew I shouldn't had done.

But with hospitals came the law, and dealing with police wasn't something I was in the mood for. In reality, it was something I would never do. Being violated in the way that I did would fuck with me for a long time, but it was a part of the game. Sometimes, you won and sometimes you lost, but being a sex worker came with risk and, unfortunately, it's what I signed up for.

She passed me her phone, and I dialed Frost's number for the last time. It rang for what seemed to be forever. Just when I was about to hang up, a female's voice answered his phone. This nigga was so bold; he really had this girl answering his phone, and that was something that he didn't even let me do. It clearly was pressure behind their relationship, which brought me closer to reality and pushed him far from my thoughts. It was the signs I couldn't ignore that was telling me to completely let go and leave him alone.

"They didn't answer," I lied, passing the phone back to her.

"Do you need a ride?" She questioned.

"No, thank you. You've done enough to help me and I couldn't thank you enough for saving my life," I answered.

"Now, if you ever need a place to lay or any form of help, don't hesitate to reach out to me at any point or time," she replied.

"Why are you helping me? Who are you?" I asked. She was way too kind, and I wanted to know if she had any other motives besides the help that she provided.

"My name is Grace, and you remind me of my daughter. She was homeless and turned to drugs… she died three years ago, and I've been helping women on the streets ever since," she responded.

"Why didn't you help your daughter?" I interrogated. It was just crazy that she didn't save her daughter's life but was trying to save mine.

"My daughter was in a bad relationship; her ex abused

her and fed her drugs. When he was done draining her of her energy, he put her out on the streets… I couldn't help her because she never reached out for help and, when I searched for her, it was hard. She was way in Vegas," she explained.

"I'm sorry about your daughter Grace," I comforted.

"Take care of yourself," she replied.

FROSTY

My phone was ringing nonstop. Mocha was being extra weird and a complete buzz to my life. She continuously bothered me when I told her not to. Icelynn answered her call and she didn't do shit other than hang up. I know she felt dumb to consistently press the issue and nothing came out of it. Genuinely, I was satisfied with Ice. We were getting money together and she was supportive.

When I laid my eyes on Ice in the club, I could tell that her aura was different and she was the complete opposite of what I was used to. Icelynn was the type of woman my mother would love. She carried the traits a woman should have. That's what I needed. I didn't want to be in the game forever.

I knew that Ice was going to be the one to take me out of the game. For once in my life, settling down didn't sound half bad.

Having a family and going legit sounded like something every man should want for themselves. It was no greater feeling than walking in the door and seeing Ice and Keaira. It was becoming something that warmed my heart and softened me up.

This Christmas was going to be a special one. Ice passed the torch to me when she opened up her life to me. She was used to doing everything alone and by herself but, this time around, I would be making sure she enjoyed hers. Being a single mother couldn't be easy. She had little to no support and that shit was bound to change.

Carrying the Christmas tree into the house, she and Keaira was in for a surprise. Yesterday, they both said they wanted a tall tree to decorate pink and white. So, I drove around the city until I found the biggest tree. I was excited to see the look on their faces this Christmas. For some reason, I was in the holiday spirit. Maybe it was the love that was in the air. A cold nigga like me was turning soft, and that was crazy.

My phone began buzzing. It was none other than Ceddy. "This shit better be good," I answered. Talking about meaningless shit would piss me off right now, especially while I was trying to go spend time with my shorty.

"We got a new shipment," Ced replied.

"Word? What it's looking like?" I questioned.

"Straight cream, come through," he answered.

"Bet, tell niggas to prepare for the re-up. I'm about to handle some shit and I'll be right there," I replied. I think it was time to put Icelynn in the game. She was ready and she did well on her first real night of hustling the club scene.

"I'm gone get the word out bro... be smooth," Ced responded before hanging up.

Pulling up in front of Ice's house, I noticed an unfamiliar car parked in front of the house. She didn't tell me that she'd be having company today. As I was carrying the tree to the porch, the door swung open. Ice was looking fine as wine in her holiday pajamas. She was holding a coffee mug in her hand with her hair tied up. I loved to see her in her natural state. She always looked the best with no makeup.

"Hey baby, I was just about to go check the mailbox," she said.

"Who car is that?" I questioned.

"My best friend, Cristal," she answered. She never introduced me to any of her friends, nor brought up names in conversation. The name sounded familiar, but I wasn't sure. Hopefully, she wasn't a female that attempted to fuck with me in the past.

The name sounded familiar, but I wasn't sure. "Oh alright, where Kiara?" I questioned.

"She upstairs playing with her god brother," Ice answered.

"Have her come down, I have something for y'all," I said as I placed the tree in the living room.

"You got us a tree? You do know I was about go buy one, right? Babe, you didn't have to," she responded in shock.

"Go get my baby, I'm about grab something from the car," I responded, walking out the front door. I grabbed the bags of decorations and gift wrap out of the trunk and brought them inside the house. The sound of Kiara's happiness brought joy over me. "Look what I got for you and mommy," I said, holding up the Target bags.

"Oh Lord, Frost! What's in there?" Ice questioned.

"Just the decorations for the tree… baby said she wanted some pink, so I got everything pink in that motherfucka," I chuckled.

"Damn, girl, he's a keeper." Icelynn's friend smiled, approaching us.

"Cristal, this is my man Frost… Frost, this is my best friend Cristal," Ice introduced.

"Nice to meet you." She smiled.

"Nice to meet you too," I replied. Cristal use to dance at the club, that's where I knew her from. If I could vaguely remember, she was one of Mocha's friends.

"Baby, thank you! This was really sweet," Ice said while wrapping her arms around my torso, hugging me.

"It's good ma," I replied, pulling out a stack from my pockets and placing it in her hands. If I was taking care of things, I did exactly that, especially fucking with a female with kids.

"What's this for?" He questioned.

"For you to pay your babysitter and go shopping for baby girl," I answered.

"Thank you, baby," she replied, hugging onto me.

"It's good mamas. I got to go handle a little business," I informed her.

"Okay, I'll see you later baby. Let me know if you need anything," she replied, walking me to the door.

Pulling her into a deep kiss, our tongues wrestled before we said our final goodbyes. That girl had my mind gone. I couldn't help but crave for her as bad as a fat bitch wanting some chocolate cake. I hopped in the car and made my way to the ghetto. It was time to bag talk. This luxury lifestyle cost, no matter how bad I wanted out.

THE SHIPMENT WAS JUST WHAT I NEEDED IT TO BE. WE HAD MORE than enough to triple the recent loss. Icelynn had the club on lock, and I had the streets on freeze. This time of year, everyone wanted drugs and definitely had the money for them. We had not only coke but also pills and bricks of promethazine on deck. We all were eating this season; it was a trappa's holiday.

"It's feeling Christmas around this motherfucka." Ced smiled.

"It sure in the fuck is! Nigga, this is what the fuck I'm talking about right here," I replied, overjoyed. Santa got my letter and gave a nigga what he needed at the right price.

"Aye niggas, I'm feeling generous… pick your poison and hit them blocks," I announced. Niggas hopped up either grabbing a key or a brick. I didn't give a fuck who sold what, as long as this shit was selling and my cut was to me when it was supposed to.

"Tell Kev to hit Central with them bricks," I demanded. Promethazine was easier to push on that side than it was over here. We were locked in with niggas on that side anyways.

"I fasho think that we can move them pills in the club fast too," Ced suggested. He wasn't lying. Half of the dancers there were doing pills or powder anyways.

"I agree, give me two bottles of Percs and those ecstasy pills," I instructed. He passed them to me.

My trust for Ice was different. She was the type of woman that I didn't see doing no weird shit. Getting hooked on drugs was something that I didn't see in her deck of cards neither. She had something to live for, her daughter. Icelynn was an amazing woman off tops, that's how I knew she was the type of woman that should be a part of my life.

"Alright brah, I'm up out of here. Yall niggas be smooth and get this shit sold and up outta here," I stated before walking out the trap.

I had a couple of stops to make before heading back to my girl. I wanted to get her a pre-Christmas gift. It sounded corny in my head but made a lot of sense to me. I hit the mall first and stopped a Kay's Jewelers. I purchased her a white gold diamond Cuban link chain along with a bracelet to match.

My next stop was to this local dog breeder who sold French bulldogs. I wanted to gift her with the rawest dog that would match her personality. My eyes met a honey golden colored female Frenchie. She looked just as feisty as my girl, and I could see that she was spoiled just like Ice ass.

After my purchases, I made my way back to my house to nap, shower, and tuck some money. Street niggas needed to unwind and reset too. Shit, it was a part of self-care. I enjoyed my peace when I had but, sometimes, the loneliness was overwhelming. Since I was young, loneliness was the part of my life that I didn't really enjoy. My mom worked really hard to provide for me, and most of those times required her to be gone for periods of a time to make sure we had a roof or food. I appreciated the struggle; it was a part of who I was and why I was the hustling ass nigga that I was. It wasn't shit wrong with that. The street motivation was what kept me going, that's the reason why I was dropping bags on single mothers in the projects every chance I got.

After my nap, I checked my phone to see a missed call from Icelynn. She called me fifteen minutes before I woke up. Before returning her calls, the texts from Mocha caught my attention. She'd been blowing me up for hours. Paragraph after paragraph explaining to me how much she loved me and why she had to leave me alone. It was annoying as hell; I didn't care about her life and what she had going on anymore. Mocha was messy and miserable. Respectfully, I blocked her number.

"Hello?" I answered as soon as Icelynn's name popped up across my screen.

"I thought you were coming back?" Icelynn questioned.

"I am baby, I have something to do." I answered.

"I need to talk to you about something," she responded.

I felt the uneasiness in her voice as though she was worried about something. I didn't want her feeling like I wasn't going to come back or like I was avoiding her. A nigga was really tired.

"Are you okay?" I questioned, trying to check the temperature.

"I'm good babe… just come home," she responded.

"Bet mami," I said before hanging up.

She didn't have to ask me twice, I was coming. Soon as the call ended, I jumped my ass out the bed and put some clothes on. It was about time to talk about our relationship and take us to the next level anyways. I was really fucking with Ice. She was nothing but a dope ass woman with dope vibes. The more time we spent together, the closer we became. Sometimes, the shit with her felt so unreal, like I wasn't used to things being too right. It made me feel like something bad was going to happen immediately after. Ice was just too calm and unproblematic to the point it did feel unreal.

Learning to accept genuine love and energy when it was presented to me was something that I was learning to do and opening myself up to it. Having a woman in my life that didn't want shit from me but my energy and time was a blessing when most women only fucked with me because I was the nigga with motion. That shit got exhausting; the happiness resided with whom I was building it with.

It took me exactly thirty minutes to get to my shorty. Before ringing the doorbell, I sat the puppy's kennel on the porch and grabbed the rest of the stuff I got for her from the trunk. Once I had everything, I rang the bell, anticipating her beautiful smile to greet me. Instead, the door swung open and I was greeted by Mocha's dirty ass.

"What the fuck is you doing here?" I snapped, ready to pull my gun out on her ass.

"I've been trying to figure that out too… this bitch didn't want to talk until you got here," Ice answered.

Just when I thought that this bitch had grown up, she showed me that she didn't. How the fuck did she even find out where Ice lived?

"Man, why are you here bro?" I questioned as I stepped into the house.

"You not happy to see me?" she questioned.

Was this bitch being for real right now? She had to be high off the snow.

"Bruh, this shit is getting out of control. How the fuck you get this address?" I questioned, as Ice burned a hole in my face with her eyes. If looks could kill, I'd be dead as day.

"Frost, I'm pregnant and I know that it's your baby… I just found out the dates add up and all," Mocha rambled, causing my mouth to drop.

This bitch was lying like fuck and clearly seeking attention that I wasn't going to give her. Delusion was definitely at an all-time high, and the fact that she even came to my girl's house with this shit knowing where I laid was crazy. I didn't have too much of anything to really say to this bitch and the look plastered across Icelynn's face was showing me how disgusted she was. Hell, even I was loss for words and disgusted. I wasn't the type of nigga to leave a bitch at the joint with my kid. That shit wasn't right, neither was it fair to her or my kid, if I did have one coming.

"Mocha, why would you bring this shit here? You could've called my phone brah," I snapped.

"You wasn't answering the phone when I was calling you, Frost… I have been dealing with hella shit and you know our bond is better than what the fuck it has been," she replied.

"I told you that you can't be on no weird shit fucking with my personal life… I am with Icelynn now. Ain't no fucking repairing bro," I explained.

"So, you chose this bitch over your family for real?" Mocha questioned, raising her voice.

"Listen bitch, you popping up to my door was already disrespectful as hell, and it just keep getting worse. I tried to spare you for the sake of your imaginary pregnancy… but you got one more time to disrespect me under my roof," Ice threatened, putting Mocha right in her place.

"This between me and Frost," Mocha snapped.

"It's about to be about my fist going upside your raggedy ass head," Ice said, stepping closer to her.

"Baby, let me handle this," I responded, grabbing Mocha by her arm. I pulled her out my girl's house; she shouldn't had even made it off the porch. "What in the fuck is your problem bro?" I questioned, dragging her to the car by her arm.

"My problem is you! Walking around here and parading with this bitch like you're happy and in love is crazy!" she snapped.

"This shit is because I'm with somebody else? Why can't

you just accept the fact that I'm done? You lie so fucking much; are you even pregnant for real?" I questioned, applying pressure to this situation as much as I could so, if she were lying, I'd see that shit right through her eyes.

"Are you serious Frost?" Mocha questioned.

"Very," I answered, as her eyes watered up. She was ridiculous as hell; it wasn't shit I did to make her feel otherwise. The audacity of her to come out the blue claiming that she was pregnant knowing that she was out here being one of the biggest hoes in the city.

"Merry Christmas nigga, you got a baby on the way!" she snapped, hopping into her car.

"If you think I won't be running a DNA test, you crazy and if I find out you using that shit while you pregnant... I'm taking that baby and gaining full custody," I informed her.

"You think they gone let a drug dealer raise a baby?" she questioned.

"It's you thinking that a dope head is more capable than a dealer... get off my girl property before I blow yo shit back!" I answered.

"Watch who the fuck you playing with Frost!" Mocha snapped.

This chick was crazier than the law allowed. She ain't have no motion to make threats. These females were fucking weird, fumbling the good ones and, when we moved on, they be crawling back.

I was stressed at this point. There was no way this girl was pregnant and, of course, I had to smooth things over with Ice. This shit was too much too soon. My girl being dragged into some unnecessary ass shit that she didn't belong in. That was some drama that I never wanted for any woman that I was dealing with, especially the one I was seeing a future with. If it wasn't one thing with Mashanti, it was another. The little game she tried playing would come to an end. I didn't understand if some shit was over between us, why couldn't she let it go? I know a nigga dick wasn't that good. Then, again, maybe it was. Mashanti wasn't the only lunatic after the Frost experience.

ICELYNN

Calling my man phone was one thing, but popping up to my house was a whole other ball game. I didn't too much care about any bitch harassing him, but popping up to where me and my kid laid was fucking insane. I didn't play with bitches and I didn't like when bitches played with me. Mocha didn't know me from a can of paint, so finding out where my daughter and I laid our heads sent me into a rage. When a bitch could stalk someone down like this, you really didn't know what they were capable of for real. While Frost continued the conversation outside, I was putting my sneakers on, preparing to whoop this bitch ass before work. If she thought an ass whooping wasn't coming, she was crazy. Just when I zipped my sweater up, Frost was walking in the door looking just as agitated as I was.

"Where are you going, Ice?" Frost asked, as I began tossing my hair into a messy bun.

Answering him was pointless when he already knew the vibes.

"Ice... I'm not talking to myself," Frost stated.

"That bitch didn't pop up at my door by herself either... now did she?" I sassed. He needed to get the hell out of my face. I really wasn't in the mood for any of his bullshit and drama that I didn't ask for.

"I'm not arguing with you, Icelynn. If you want to talk, we can do that, but all the petty shit you're doing needs to fucking stop," he snapped.

"I'm going to work Frost... stay here if you want to. I don't give a fuck," I snapped, brushing past him.

Frost grabbed me by my arm and pushed me against the wall gently.

"We're about to talk, you're not walking out of here with attitude," Frost said in a very stern tone.

Instantly, I rolled my eyes and walked into the living room. As I sat on the couch, he watched my every move before sitting next to me. My attitude was through the roof and I knew he felt that shit from just sniffing the air. One thing that grinded my gears was problematic shit. I wasn't a problematic bitch.

"I don't want no problems babe and this shit right here

will never happen again. One thing I'd never want is for you to be in the midst of some random ass shit, especially over me. My apologies, you have every right to feel the ways that you do," Frost said.

Of course, it wasn't his fault that his ex was hella salty. I just didn't do drama; I'd never had to and I wasn't going to start.

"I accept your apology but understand that this isn't something 1 want to deal with. The randomness and the drama was so uncalled for… popping up to my house was even more insane," I responded.

"It was and it's going to get handled. I don't believe that she's pregnant either and, if she is, I'm sure that it's not mine," he stated. He didn't have to say that shit just to make me feel better. I didn't feel any type of way about him and his possible baby mama bullshit. It was his past, it had nothing to do with me.

"Don't just be saying that shit to say it… if that's your baby, take care of it," I replied.

"If it's mine, I will, but her ass is lying," he replied.

"I've gotta go to work," I said, trying my hardest to ignore this conversation. I didn't feel like discussing his possible child.

"Are we good?" he questioned, looking me dead in the eyes as if he was trying to peep into my soul.

This nigga made it impossible to stay mad. From his eyes to his skin, I was hella mesmerized. It made me the two W's, wet and weak.

"We good Frost," I responded, trying to ignore the signals my body was sending.

"I got a new pack for you, it's already cut and bagged," he informed me.

"Okay. You coming to the club tonight?" I questioned him.

"No, I got eyes on you, though. Take my car and leave yours," he instructed.

"Why can't I drive my own car?" I questioned.

"What's wrong with my car?" he questioned. Just like a nigga to answer a question with a question.

"It's a gun in the glove compartment, if you need it… use it," Frost added.

"Okay, give me a kiss," I demanded before grabbing my bag, along with the product.

He pulled me by my waist and kissed me deeply before pulling away. Tomorrow was Christmas Eve. I wanted to be home in time to wrap Kiara's gifts while she was with her godmother, Cristal.

"Before you go, I want to give you something." Frost smiled, reaching into a gift bag. He revealed a jewelry box. Once it opened, my eyes instantly widened. It was the most beautiful Cuban link chain. It held a heart shaped pendant iced the fuck out.

"Frost… this for me?" I questioned.

"Of course, so is that puppy over there," he answered.

I was so annoyed that I didn't even realize he walked in here with this animal. When people dropped their fucked-up ass energies into your home, it was bound to throw you off.

"Thank you so much baby. When I come home tonight… I'm sucking the skin off your dick," I promised. Frost continued spoiling me in ways I'd never been before. It was far from his money; it was his time and his patience, as well as the energy he had been pouring into me.

"I'm going to meet you at the club in two hours," Frost responded. We gave each other another kiss before I dipped out.

THE CLUB WAS FIRED UP. EVERY TIME I STEPPED IN THIS motherfucker was turned the fuck up entirely. Mocha's trifling ass was nowhere to be found and I was glad for the sake of this "pregnancy" she claimed to be going through. The whole thing seemed fabricated to me. That was just my opinion and, if she thought that I was going to allow her to pull a wool over my man's eyes, she truly had another thing coming.

Bitches in the club were so envious of me to the point where it didn't make any sense. Some looked up to me and some had been carrying this stank ass energy since I walked in here on my first day. Me giving a fuck was impossible. These whores didn't mean shit to me; I was here to accumulate a bag and nothing more. Moving Frost's product through the club made me a lot of money and the way that I was doing it was discreet. Nobody would know shit unless somebody opened their mouth to the wrong person.

"Bitch, you think you somebody special?" Trix questioned, walking up on me with a switchblade. I know this bitch was crazy out her mind walking up on me with a damn weapon.

"Trix are for kids, hoe, get the fuck out my face," I chuckled, turning my attention to counting my money.

"I ain't going nowhere. I don't like you," she responded, stepping closer. She said that as if I was supposed to care.

"Do I look like I care? Stand in line with the others," I laughed as I continued thumbing through each dollar.

"You walk up in my club taking my regulars? I will beat your ass… you taking money from my kids' mouths bitch! I have five kids," she explained.

"Twenty-seven with five kids sounds crazy but, if you want to make some side money, let me know mamas," I replied, not taking my eyes off my dough.

"You think you funny hoe?" Trix questioned.

Before I could respond, my man entered the dressing room and she walked off.

"You good baby?" Frost questioned.

"I'm great… that little hoe is just mad as hell with her raggedy ass," I laughed, wrapping my stacks with the rubber bands.

"I'm gonna be waiting for you outside, you sure you good?" Frost questioned. He stepped for me in every way each time, that man ain't playing about me.

"I'm great, not worried about no bitch bringing a knife to a gun fight," I chuckled.

He grabbed me by my neck and kissed me. "Crazy ass, hurry up," he demanded.

As his wish was my command, I hurriedly got myself dressed and grabbed my bags, walking through the club. Just when I walked out, confetti dropped everywhere and the DJ changed the record.

"Congratulations to the new club owner, Ice! Make some motherfucking noise for the head bitch in charge!" the DJ hollered into the mic, taking me by complete surprise.

How the fuck was I the club owner? This had to be a fucking joke. Everyone clapped and cheered, yet I was the only one still puzzled. Just then, Frost approached me with a big ass bouquet of roses and a golden key. I knew right then he was responsible for this.

"Congratulations, boss lady, this club is yours and all these bitches hating on you are now your workers." He smiled.

This nigga was the one for me hands down.

"I love you, Frost," I admitted. It was my truth though. I didn't care how soon or fast it was, the heart wanted what the heart wanted. He was truly pouring into me in ways I couldn't ever imagine a man could.

"Ma, I love you too, I got us," he responded.

"How did you make this happen?" I asked.

"Just know the world is yours, we are just living in it... let's go home!" he answered.

With no hesitation, we were dipping out. Frost didn't even know how much pussy I'd be throwing at him tonight.

"Merry Christmas baby." Frost smiled before pulling me

into the most passionate kiss I've ever had. He was mothing but good to me and, for once in my life, I felt whole and complete. At last, I felt peace within our bond.

"Merry Trapmas babe," I responded, passing him the duffel bag full of cash as we walked out of my first establishment hand in hand.

Did you enjoy the read?
Let us know how much by leaving us a review on Amazon
and Goodreads.

PREVIEW

Keep reading for a preview of…

Melted the Heart of a Menace

By P. Wise

TREASURE "TINK" KING

"Lay still, damnit," I snapped at my best friend Maleah.

I was doing her recovery massage. We had just gotten back from Miami a week before, where she got her BBL done.

"It hurts like hell, Tink," she cried, calling me by my nickname. Tears were literally making their escape from her eyes.

"I told you this wasn't going to be no easy shit," I reminded her.

When it came to having cosmetic surgery, the actual procedure was the easy part; the recovery was what needed to be worried about. Everyone's pain tolerance was different so, when getting the massages, I always got different reactions.

"I know, Tink, damn," she snapped at me out of anger.

She was acting like I placed a gun to her head and told her to go and get her body done. Once she saw I got mine done and I had no complaints, she wanted to go ahead and give it a shot.

Maleah was my childhood best friend. We both grew up on the same block in Bed-Stuy, Brooklyn and attended the same school from grade level all the way to high school. She was my right-hand and been a loyal friend since day one. Out of our crew that consisted of four of us, she was my main bitch.

"One more roll and we're finished. Let's just get it over with," I tried to persuade her.

She squeezed her eyes shut tightly and took a deep breath in and out. "Okay, go ahead."

I went on and quickly finished her session, so she could get out my massage room with her cry baby self.

After I experienced getting my body done, I saw the importance of recovery and post operation. I went to school, studied therapeutics massage and beauty and became a licensed massage therapist and esthetician. After taking on a few clients and gaining more experience, I landed a job at Body Right LLC in Brooklyn where I worked for the past three years.

Body Right LLC was where all the ladies came after going through cosmetic surgery to get their recovery massages and more. Plus, it was a comforting place to many when it came to all their massage, body care, and relaxing needs.

"Whew, thank God, it's over," Maleah exclaimed, looking relieved.

"Girl." I side-eyed her and curled my lip up. She was so extra when she wanted to be.

"So, how are things with Justin?" she pried, referring to my boyfriend of two years.

Justin Jenkins was my on and off-again boyfriend. We lived together, but it didn't feel like it at times. He would stay out all night and, sometimes, even days would past and he wouldn't make it home. His excuse was he was on the road jugging and making money for us. I knew what I had signed up for two years prior when we got together. The nice threads, date and club nights were lit in my eyes. That was before I really understood what I needed in a man. At the time we met, I was dealing with trying to balance life and my mother dying from cancer.

Justin was an outlet and was helping out with a lot when it came to my bills and my mother's medical expenses. While he kept me satisfied financially in some sort of way, I yearned for more of his time, especially since I knew he was out in the streets fuckin' on hoes.

"Things are cool. Can't complain," I simply put. Even though Maleah was my girl, I just knew better than to speak too much on my personal business.

As soon as I was finished with her, I attended to my other client who was prepped and waiting for me. My client had already passed the beginning stages of healing, so her session went by quick; I was literally in and out.

When I left out the room to head to the front by the waiting area, I saw my boss, Sarena, smelling a bouquet of roses at the front desk.

"Awwwhhh, that's so sweet," I sang. "Who's it from?"

"Oh, this dude I just started talking to; he's a sweetheart with deep pockets," she stated while smiling at the roses.

"Oh yeah? You can never go wrong with one of those."

"At all, he's even talking about helping me expand the business."

Hearing her say those words got me upset a bit. It wasn't anything towards her, it was towards Justin. For the longest time, he kept promising me that he was going to help me open my own spa and recovery home. Time and time again as I tried my best to save up and start the process, he would come up with excuses; it was discouraging as fuck.

"Good for you." I smiled.

Moments later, Maleah walked to the waiting area dressed and ready to go. "Alright, bye friend. I'll see you tomorrow for Thanksgiving, right?"

Shit, I forgot, I thought.

"Yup, sure will," I confirmed because I had no other choice.

We hugged one another goodbye, and I returned to work.

THANKSGIVING DAY...

"Hands on your knees (ho), hands on your knees (ow). Shake that ass for Drake (yup), now, shake that ass for me," Sexyy Red rapped her verse on *Rich Baby Daddy* by Drake, featuring her and SZA.

The girls and I were shaking our ass and having a time

after we filled our bellies with everything a person could imagine having for Thanksgiving. Despite getting into it with Justin earlier that day about us not spending time for the holiday knowing it was a hard one for me, I tried to enjoy myself. My girls knew how to get me out of a funky ass mood, which was why I appreciated them a lot.

A year before, I spent Thanksgiving with my mother and Justin. It was just us three at home, munching and laughing. That Thanksgiving was the last one I would ever spent with my moms. She passed the following month on Christmas day.

The holidays used to be the most exciting time in my life but, after losing her, it just didn't feel right celebrating without her. My girls were aware of everything, hence the reason they tried to keep me active and happy. Justin, on the other hand, felt making money was more important than spending time with me on a day like that.

"Alright y'all, I'm finna dip. I'm tired than a mudda," I joked in a Jamaican accent.

"How you gon' get home? Let me drive you," Maleah offered.

"No, stay and have fun. I'll take an Uber."

"You sure?"

"Yes, I'm positive, girl."

I grabbed my phone and requested a ride and, just my luck, one accepted and was only three minutes away. Gathering my belongings, I slipped into my winter coat and grabbed my things. Quickly saying my goodbyes to the girls, I made my way downstairs to meet my ride.

As soon as I reached the front stoop, he pulled up. Before walking up to the car, I matched the license plates from the one on the app to his car. Too much bullshit was happening in the world not to take proper precaution.

I slid into the backseat and got comfortable, as the driver pulled off toward my place. Scrolling through my social medias, I looked at all the happy couples that were out enjoying each other and couldn't help but feel a sting of jealousy. I just didn't know what it was gon' take for Justin to act right.

Quickly, I went deep into my thoughts about him and our relationship, thinking about how things were in the beginning and how they had changed. I analyzed my actions and what I could've done to better the situation, but I damn near came up empty on suggestions.

Bang!

Off the huge impact, my body was tossed to the other side of the backseat as my head smashed against the window. My vision became blurred, but I still had some kind of consciousness. I reached for my bag to get my phone but a wave of pain hit me, causing me to faint back onto the seat.

I heard voices near the car and instantly felt some relief to know we were going to be saved. The driver wasn't moving, nor did he say a word, so I knew he was knocked out unconscious or, worst, dead.

Someone was tugging at the doors and finally pried them open. Still with a blurred vision, I tried to see, but it was still hard.

"Aye, it's a joint in here," I heard a guy say.

"Damn, he was on a ride," another one stated. "Fuck it, we gotta grab her too."

Huh, what? I thought.

As soon as I felt hands grabbing on me and pulling me out of the vehicle, panic set in. I had no clue what the hell was going on, so the first thing that came to mind was to kick and scream.

"Stop, please, stop! Get off me!" I pleaded, as they got me out of the car and over one of their shoulders.

Hollering at the top of my lungs, I was shoved in the back of a trunk with nothing but a fearful feeling. Immediately after, someone else was pushed into the trunk beside me, which I assumed was the driver. The door was slammed closed.

"Help, please, help!" I screamed as I kicked at the door with all my might. My body was in so much pain but, at that moment, I didn't care.

We drove some ways and, after a while, when I saw I was hollering for no reason, I just stopped and cried to myself. The person next to me was still out and hadn't moved an inch.

When we finally stopped, I heard doors opening and closing, then footsteps coming and stopping at the trunk. I felt around for anything I could've used to hit them with, but the trunk was completely empty. Once the door opened, almost immediately, they placed something over my head and I saw nothing but darkness, followed by tape being stuck over my mouth.

Lifted out the trunk and over someone's shoulder, I gave a

hard time once again. But my little frame was no match for the brolic ass man that was carrying me.

"Chill the fuck out, yo," he growled.

Hearing the tone of his voice and him squeezing my thigh hard made me keep quiet, for the moment that was.

We entered what I assumed was a building of some kind because I no longer felt the biting cold winds. He carried me down some steps and down a hall. Placing me down on a cold concrete floor, I heard him quickly shuffle out of the room and close the door.

I snatched the bag off my head since they never bounded my hands and took a look around. My vision still wasn't a hundred percent clear, but it was better. The Uber driver was lying next to me motionless and still. When I didn't hear anyone outside of the room door, I went ahead and tried to wake him up.

"Hey, hey, are you okay?" I asked as I gave his body a couple of nudges. After I saw he wasn't responding, I checked his pulse to see if he was alive or dead, but he was still breathing, thankfully.

I heard footsteps coming my way, and the door flung open with a few guys wearing skully masks. They rushed in and separated the driver and me, dragging us on opposite sides of the room.

"What's this about? Please, let me go," I pleaded.

Two guys carried a large bucket of water and stepped in front of the driver. Seconds later, they poured the water down on him, causing him to jump out of his unconsciousness.

"What the fuck?" he asked, trying to catch his breath and bearings.

Looking around the room, he noticed we were in some deep shit. His eyes roamed from the guys and then to me. While most of the men were inside of the room with us, one stood by the door in a calm manner. I continued to watch him from the corner of my eyes, but I noticed he kept his attention on me.

"Where that package you were supposed to drop off two days ago?" one of the guys bent down to his eye level and asked.

"What, what package?" the driver stuttered.

The guy hung his head and grabbed the gun from his waistline. "Where the fuck is the package, David Rice?" he asked again, that time calling his government name; I remembered seeing his name on the Uber app.

"Fuck," David whispered to himself but loud enough for everyone to hear. "I so-so-sold it."

"Nigga, you sold five bricks? Aye Tee, I think you need to get his ass on the team," the guy joked as he spoke to the one standing in the doorway. "Where the fuck the money at then?"

"I'll tell you, just please don't kill me," David bargained.

"Man, where the shit at?"

"It's at my place, under my bed," he informed them.

The guy turned and looked at the other one by the door, who then gave him a head nod, prompting him to move away from David. Within that very second, he stood to the side, and a bullet was lodged in the center of David's head; I almost lost my shit. My body shook vigorously as my whole life flashed before me.

"What we doing with her?" he asked the guy, who lowered his gun and started to walk away.

He turned around and looked at me for a moment. "Off her," he stated in a nonchalant tone.

"Nooo!" I shouted with tears in my eyes. "Please don't. I won't say anything. I don't even know how y'all look."

They all just stood there looking at me beg for my life, and I didn't give a fuck how I looked. Snotty nose and all, they were going to feel me. The quiet one, which I assumed to be the boss since he was calling the shots, walked over to me and squatted down.

"How I know you not just saying anything to get up outta here?" he asked.

"You don't know that, but I pray you give me a chance. I promise, this never happened."

"Chances get you killed and, in my case, could get us locked the fuck up."

"That won't happen because I don't know shit."

I searched his eyes for any sign of humanity while I noticed him searching mine for what I believed was to see if I was being truthful, which I was. "Please, I don't wanna die like this," I cried.

"So, how do you want to die?" He continued to stare at me without blinking.

"I don't know but not anytime soon."

"Man, let her go, Tee. We'll just keep an eye on her," the shooter spoke.

"Where her shit at?" Tee asked, remembering his name.

One guy grabbed my bag that was in the room's corner and handed it to Tee. He started to looking through it and found my wallet with my ID card and work badge.

"Treasure Issa Naami King. What a long fuckin' name," he ridiculed, chuckling afterwards. Taking pictures of them, he slipped the contents back into my wallet and placed it back inside my bag.

"Listen, Treasure, as you know, I can kill you right now. But because I feel a little generous and my boy suggested I let you go, I'll do so. But I will be watching you and, if you even think about opening up your mouth, I will make sure you die slowly just because you didn't keep your word. We got an understanding?"

I nodded my head quickly as I felt myself choking up.

"Words, Treasure, I need to hear you say it."

"We have an understanding. You have my word," I confirmed.

"Good girl."

He stood up and walked out of the room, never looking back. The same bag that was on my head when I was carried in was back covering my vision as I felt them pick me up off the ground. That time around, there was no kicking and screaming, but I still felt angst knowing they could've easily changed their minds.

I was placed in the backseat of a vehicle different from my arrival, but I had no complaints. My mouth was shut but my mind was racing a thousand miles per hour while I prayed I made it home safely.

A few days had passed since the whole ordeal. My body was hurting from the accident and my mind had been playing tricks on me. Any time I closed my eyes, I saw David slumped against the wall with a bullet in his head. After the smoked cleared, someone trained the gun on me and, any time I heard a shot being fired, I would jump out of my sleep.

Monday rolled around faster than I could think. I had a few days to stay in the bed and try to get myself together. Justin wasn't home all weekend, which for once I was actually happy about that. I didn't have to explain why I came home so late after Friendsgiving with the girls or why I was bruised up and startled by every little noise I heard.

Knowing I had to act normal and like nothing happened, I rolled out of my bed and got dressed to head into work. I knew it would've taken some time for me to get my mind off things and, while doing so, I had to keep a straight face.

When I arrived at work, I went about my day as usual. I took clients and walk-ins just to keep myself distracted from drowning in my thoughts. Anytime I went outside for a little fresh air, I felt like someone was watching me. They said they were going to keep eyes on me, but I didn't think they were literally going to do so. But understanding the severity of the crime, I might've done the same.

"Tink!" I heard my boss yell out to me.

I was in my room just chilling before my next client came. I had a good hour before the appointment. "Yeah, I'm coming!" I hollered back as I left out the room and made my way to the front.

A fine, light skinned guy was standing at the receptionist's desk. From what I could see, he had tattoos all on his neck and the side of his head. He wore a low cut but had a Fendi winter hat on. His threads were expensive and he looked to be about six feet in height, which was tall to me since I stood at only five-two.

"This gentleman would like to get a full body massage. Can you take him before your four o'clock?" Serena asked.

I wasn't doing shit but scrolling on social media, and a distraction was what I needed. When I looked at him closer, he looked familiar, but I couldn't put my finger on where I knew him from.

"Sure, come with me." I motioned for him to follow me to the back.

When we got in the room, I gave him instructions to take off his clothes, except for his boxers, and lie on the bed. Then, I instructed him to cover his lower half with the towel I provided him with. I couldn't help but to scan his body as it was tatted from every angle possible. His entire chest, stomach, back, and arms, even his right leg, was riddled with art work.

I dimmed the lights and turned on the music softly to get the vibe going. My clients being comfortable while I worked on them was important. I wanted to take them to another place while they were in my care. Starting his massage, I oiled his skin down nicely. My hand passed on his back, feeling a huge scar that lined from the top to the side of his stomach.

Looking at the mark reminded me of a situation that happened to someone I knew as a kid. He was sliced in that same spot; I remembered it like it had just been the day prior.

Shaking my thoughts, I continued to massage his body from head to toe. When he came in, he was tense but, by the time I was finished with him, he was relaxed. I had that effect on everyone that I touched.

"I'll step out, so you can get dressed," I told him as I exited out the door.

To kill a few minutes, I went and used the bathroom, then made my rounds to check on my co-workers on my way back to my room. When I got back, I knocked on the door and waited to hear a response before walking in.

"Yo," I heard him say.

I walked in, and he was putting on his Cuban link around his neck. Since we were finally up close and he didn't have anything blocking me from seeing all of him, I noticed who it was.

"Treyce?" I asked.

He looked up at me with a blank look. "It's Trigg now," he corrected.

What I thought was a reunion quickly turned into a terrifying moment. I connected the voice, eyes, and body structure; it was the Tee guy from Thanksgiving night, someone I knew as Treyce.

Available Now

On all online retail book platforms!

OTHER BOOKS BY

<u>*MIA SKY*</u>

Falling For A Cali Boss

Welcome to Cherrieville 'Sweet Nothings'

Forever His Millennium

A BBW Valentines

Housewives of The Drug Game 'Hazel & Jaiceon'

Forever His Millennium 2

Born into The Game

Forever His Millennium 3

OTHER BOOKS BY

URBAN AINT DEAD

Tales 4rm Da Dale

The Hottest Summer Ever

By **Elijah R. Freeman**

Despite The Odds

By **Juhnell Morgan**

Good Girl Gone Rogue

By **Manny Black**

Hittaz

Hittaz 2

Hittaz 3

Coldhearted

By **Lou Garden Price, Sr.**

Charge It To The Game

Charge It To The Game 2

A Summer To Remember With My Hitta

Snatched Up By A Hitta

By **Nai**

COMING SOON FROM

URBAN AINT DEAD

The Hottest Summer Ever 2

THE G-CODE

How To Publish A Book From Prison

Tales 4rm Da Dale 2

Hittin' Licks For The Holidays

By **Elijah R. Freeman**

Hittaz 4

Coldhearted 2

By **Lou Garden Price, Sr.**

The Swipe 2

By **Toola**

Good Girl Gone Rogue 3

By **Manny Black**

Despite The Odds 2

Hittin' Licks For The Holidays: Chicago

By **Juhnell Morgan**

Charge It To The Game 3

Santa Sent Me A Real One For Christmas

By **Nai**

The State's Witness 3

By **Kyiris Ashley**

Ridin For You, Too

By **Telia**

A Setup For Revenge 2

By **Ashley Williams**

Falling For A Texas Savage

By **Juanita TheAuthor**

A Millionaire Under The Mistletoe

By **Mia Sky**

Pretti & The Beast

By **P. Wise**

BOOKS BY

URBAN AINT DEAD's C.E.O

<u>Elijah R. Freeman</u>

Triggadale

Triggadale 2

Triggadale 3

Tales 4rm Da Dale

The Hottest Summer Ever

Murda Was The Case

Murda Was The Case 2

Murda Was The Case 3

STAY CONNECTED

Follow
Elijah R. Freeman
On Social Media
FB: Elijah R. Freeman
IG: @the_future_of_urban_fiction

9 7 9 8 9 8 8 8 4 1 5 5 5